TOUGH HOMBRE

His name was Kirk Fallon. He rode tall on a buckskin horse deep into the Apache ground of Arizona—to exact payment for an ancient, bloody debt.

The law was his calling, but his business today was violence. The private kind that exploded beneath a midday sun—between two men advancing to meet each other up a narrow, dusty street that soon would be dyed red. . .

Dudley Dean was the name Dudley Dean McGaughey used from the beginning for his series of exemplary Western novels written for Fawcett Gold Medal in the 1950s. McGaughey was born in Rialto, California, and began writing fiction for Street & Smith's *Wild West Weekly* in the early 1930s under the name Dean Owen. These early stories, and many more longer pulp novels written for *Masked Rider Western* and *Texas Rangers* after the Second World War, were aimed at a youthful readership. The 1950s marked McGaughey's Golden Age and virtually all that he wrote as Dudley Dean, Dean Owen, or Lincoln Drew during this decade repays a reader with rich dividends in tense storytelling and historical realism. This new direction can be seen in short novels he wrote early in the decade such as "Gun the Man Down" in *5 Western Novels* (8/52) and "Hang the Man High!" in *Big-Book Western* (3/54). They are notable for their maturity and presage the dramatic change in tone and characterization that occur in the first of the Dudley Dean novels, *Ambush at Rincon* (1953). *The Man from Riondo* (1954), if anything, was even better, with considerable scope in terms of locations, variety of characters, and unusual events. *Gun in the Valley* (1957) by Dudley Dean, *Chainlink* (1957) by Owen Evens, and *Rifle Ranch* (1958) by Lincoln Drew are quite probably his finest work among the fine novels from this decade. These stories are notable in particular for the complexity of their social themes and psychological relationships, but are narrated in a simple, straightforward style with such deftly orchestrated plots that their subtlety and depth may become apparent only upon reflection.

TOUGH HOMBRE

Dudley Dean

GUNSMOKE

This hardback edition 2001
by Chivers Press
by arrangement with
Golden West Literary Agency

ISBN 0 7540 8143 5

British Library Cataloguing in Publication Data available

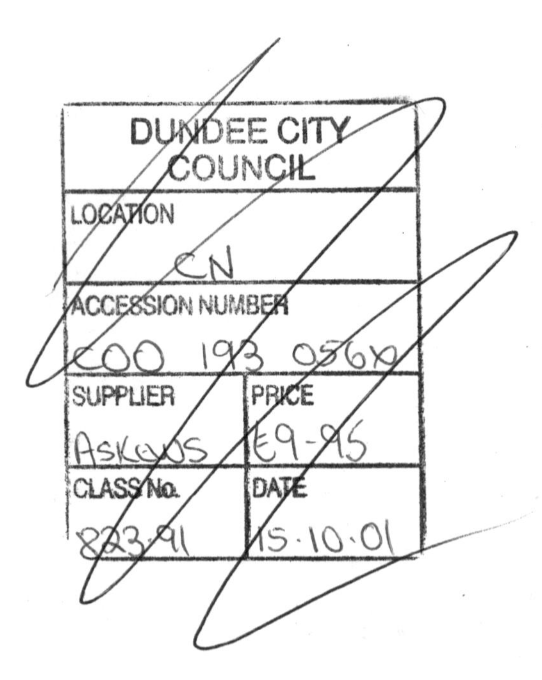

Printed and bound in Great Britain by
Bookcraft, Midsomer Norton, Somerset

Tough Hombre

Chapter One

THE TWO RIDERS pushed deeper into the Cobre Mountains, one of them intent on killing a man, the other expecting payment from the same man for injuries received and the theft of money and horses. The taller of the two men, Kirk Fallon, was the younger. He was on the short side of thirty, with gray eyes narrowed against the Arizona sun. He was a big man on a buckskin horse, his clothing showing the wear of the trail west from Kansas. More than once he had to caution his companion, the taciturn Ard Dunster, about foundering their horses in overeagerness to reach the end of a five-year trail. These mountains were no place for a man to be afoot.

Kirk rode with the brim of his black hat pulled low, scanning the jagged uplift of rock and smooth golden sea of September aspen. He watched for a smudge of camp smoke or a movement of riders.

They knew this to be the country of the Juniper Pool, a group of mountain ranchers who looked upon strangers suspiciously. This country originally had been the hunting ground of the Apache. And occasionally a band of Indians would break out of the reservation at Fort Bedloe and hang white men's hair from their belts to show their contempt for the invader.

These two were familiar with danger, one on the side of the law, the other on the side of the fence where the money was quicker and more easily spent. Ard Dunster's face reflected the pattern of his life with the gun. It was deeply grooved; his eyes were small, watching. He was forty-two years old, and since his twelfth birthday, sleeping or awake, a revolver had always been within his reach.

Again where the trail curved upward through a rocky canyon Kirk Fallon had to caution Dunster to pull up. Dunster's black horse stumbled on the shale.

"Once I meet up with Walt Chance," Dunster snapped over a narrow shoulder, "I'll buy a new horse."

Finally Dunster pulled up. Kirk was almost sorry he had let Dunster know that after five years he had found Walt Chance. He had seen Dunster only a half-dozen times during those years. But they had corresponded whenever one of them had any lead to the man they sought.

"I'm going to shoot him low," Dunster said. They had halted in the shade of junipers to let their horses drink. "Real low. I want to watch his eyes."

"Remember, I settle with him first," Kirk said.

"Sure. Then I'm going to kill the son."

Kirk stretched his long legs and tipped back his hat on his thick yellow hair.

Four years running he had inserted advertisements in frontier newspapers, and then given up on it.

$500 REWARD
for the locating of
Walt Chance, five feet
nine inches tall, black
hair and mustache. Ranched
near Santa Margarita, Chihuahua,
Mexico, in 1868. Contact Kirk
Fallon, Borden, Kansas.

Many addresses Kirk had had over the years. The Borden address was the one he had used on the last ad. Strange that it was the one that got results. It was when Kirk had given up ever finding Chance that a letter came from Pete Shatto, who ranched in the Cobre Mountains. Shatto had run across a year-old Tucson paper and seen the advertisement. Shatto wrote that for the $500 he would take Kirk to the man he was seeking. Kirk was to meet Shatto at the latter's ranch on September 15. With his letter Shatto had sent a detailed map.

Many times Kirk had followed false leads, but this time he sensed success. After all, Pete Shatto knew Chance by sight. Shatto had worked for the Barrios brothers in Chihuahua at the same time Kirk and Walt Chance and Danny Dunster, Ard Dunster's young brother, had been partners.

Walt Chance had killed Danny Dunster. He had shot Kirk in the back and left him to die.

"I figure that Chance owes me seventy-eight hundred dollars," Kirk said, when they were riding again.

"More better to put a bullet in his gut," Dunster said. "I ain't forgot he killed my brother."

Despite his years on the frontier as deputy, gun guard, ranch foreman, and—his last job—marshal of the tough cattle town of Borden, Kirk could not get used to one man calmly discussing the murder of another. For it was murder, no matter what Chance had done in that moment when greed had dictated that he dispose of his two partners. Kirk hoped that if Chance had no money to settle up, the man would at least have the nerve to pull a gun. Then Kirk would gladly kill him. But to strip a man of weapons as Dunster planned and then shoot him in the stomach was something hard to take.

They made a dry camp and ate *carne seca* and cold *tortillas*. Dunster paced the camp, impatient to kill and be on his way.

Lying in the darkness with his head on his saddle, Kirk thought of the years of his search. Five years of living for the moment when once again he would face the soft-spoken Southerner.

As Kirk stared up through the juniper branches to the glittering stars, he thought, At last I can have a life of my own. No more chasing shadows, asking the same questions at saloons, cow camps, lonely ranches: "Do you know a man named Walt Chance?" He would describe Chance. And then: "He's one of the few Americans I ever knew who favored a Chihuahua saddle."

Now the waiting was over, or nearly so. Last year Kirk had speculated on a rising cattle market. As a result his money belt was thick and heavy with four thousand dollars in gold and currency. This, coupled with the money owed him by Walt Chance, would enable him finally to put down his roots.

They had kept track of the days since leaving Kansas by tying a knot in a string for each day. Tomorrow was *the* day.

By midmorning they were through the Rim by a narrow pass Shatto had marked on the map he had sent. Then they continued on the wagon road until they saw a sorry-looking shack in the center of a littered yard. There was a barn with a storm-damaged roof, a corral in need of repair, and a shed. Two bony work horses and a mule were in the corral.

Pete Shatto was sitting on the porch, and now he came down the broken steps. He seemed surprised to see the man with Kirk. Shatto looked thinner and older and more unkempt than Kirk Fallon remembered from the days in Mexico.

"Howdy, Fallon," Shatto said, his nervous blue eyes swinging to Dunster. "Didn't figure on you comin' with anybody else. Who's this?"

Kirk introduced Dunster.

Shatto wiped the palms of his hands along his patched Levis. "Danny Dunster was a good boy," Shatto said, trying to keep his reedy voice under control. "I remember him well. So you're his brother."

"The hell with that," Dunster said coldly. "Show us Chance. That's what we come for."

Shatto cast a nervous glance toward the unpainted house. Kirk thought he caught sight of a woman's gray head at the front window, but couldn't be sure. He felt a knot of apprehension at the back of his neck.

"You're jumpy," he told Shatto. "Why?"

Shatto gave him a weak smile. "No reason. Just surprised that two of you come. I just figured on Fallon."

"Don't make a damn bit of difference," Dunster snapped. "It's more my show than Fallon's, anyhow. My brother's dead. Fallon's still walkin' around. Now quit stalling. Where's Chance?"

"Well, I got to sorta change plans, maybe."

Dunster's right hand flashed down and a gun appeared. He pushed the muzzle hard against Shatto's yellow teeth. "You'll have another mouth at the back of your head if you don't show us Walt Chance."

Shatto's long frame trembled, but he said, "I'll saddle my mule."

Kirk glanced at the cliff rising behind the house. On all sides of the clearing aspen grew thickly. "I don't like this," Kirk said under his breath.

Dunster made an impatient gesture. "I want Chance dead before the sun's gone," he said, and with a calloused thumb he lifted the hammer of his black-butted gun and slowly let it down. "Then we'll go down to El Cobre and bite the dog."

"You kill a man, then get drunk to celebrate?"

Dunster turned his cold, wedge-shaped face on Kirk. "If you don't like the way I'm doin' it," Ard Dunster said, "then stay out. I'll get Chance myself!"

"Don't try your toughness on me, Ard," Kirk Fallon warned. "I'm not Pete Shatto."

They eyed each other for a moment. Kirk was an inch under six feet. His legs, clad in dusty Levis, were long. He had a solid chunk of jaw. His hawk nose had once been broken, so that now the bridge was almost straight. His mouth was wide, showing half-moons of pressure. His gun was cedar-butted.

Dunster backed off. "Guess we're both gettin' jumpy," he said, and mounted his horse when Pete Shatto rode the mule out of the corral and turned to put the bailing-wire loop over a post to secure the gate.

"Where you takin' us?" Dunster demanded, as they rode down through the aspens, following a well-defined trail.

Shatto told them what a cinch it was going to be to get Walt Chance. Chance came regularly to a deserted line shack about five miles south. There he met the wife of a neighboring rancher.

Kirk said dubiously, "Walt Chance wasn't a woman-chaser when I knew him."

"What of it?" Dunster said impatiently.

"How do you know he'll be there today?" Kirk demanded of Shatto.

"They'll be there," Shatto said, and flashed them a weak smile. "That's why I told you to be sure and come today."

"This thing has got skunk odor," Kirk said thinly to Dunster.

Dunster made no reply. Impatience put a hard shine

in his small eyes. He kept lifting his gun and shoving it back in its holster.

"Remember," Kirk warned in a low voice as he swung beside Dunster on the narrow trail, "I want to talk to Chance first."

Dunster gave him an ugly grin, and drew from a belt scabbard a long-bladed knife. "Maybe I'll use this on him. While he's stuffin' his guts back in with his fingers you can have your talk."

The corners of Kirk's wide mouth turned down as if he had tasted something sour. "I've killed a few in my time, but I never enjoyed it. I think you do."

Shatto said over his shoulder, "You got the five hundred dollars with you?"

Kirk slapped his money belt. "I've got my share," he said, and noticed that Dunster as well as Shatto regarded the gesture with narrow-eyed interest.

For perhaps the twentieth time Kirk regretted writing Ard Dunster that Chance had been located at last. Much better had he come here alone. Dunster wasn't the sort of man for a friend. As they began climbing a trail over a hogback, Kirk tried to associate the laughing Danny Dunster he had known in Mexico with the cold-eyed brother who now rode at his side.

Shadows were lengthening across the face of the Cobres when at last they came to a canyon where a small frame building was set in a clearing.

"There it is," Shatto said, pointing a shaking finger at the shack. "You boys wait there and Chance will be along directly."

"What if the woman comes here first?" Dunster wanted to know.

Pete Shatto gave a hollow laugh. "You hate Chance so much, I reckon you wouldn't back off from having sport with his woman."

Kirk was eying Shatto's nervous face. "I don't like this, Ard," he said.

In his eagerness to settle with Chance, Dunster flung himself from his horse. "Come on, Fallon," he said, and started tramping toward the shack. "We'll look the place over, then hide the horses."

Frowning, Kirk started to swing down and follow.

Pete Shatto suddenly yelled, "Watch it, Charlie! There's *two* of 'em!"

And instantly a lank man with the same narrow face and shifty eyes as Pete Shatto's rose out of the brush. He was to the right of the shack. He held a double-barreled shotgun.

Ard Dunster snapped to a halt. "What the hell!" he said, and started a hand for his revolver.

The shotgun spat smoke and flame and whistling buckshot. Dunster went down as if hit by a scythe.

Chapter Two

A COLD TERROR gripped Kirk Fallon. He flung himself from his horse as he saw the man swing the shotgun. The man's eyes were wild with tension. His finger slipped back to the rear trigger, ready to send that tearing blast of lead at his new target. Kirk struck the ground, rolled hard, landing on his left shoulder. The shotgun roared an instant later. He heard some of the slugs scream above his prostrate body.

All the instinct he had acquired during the war and his years on the frontier congealed in one driving effort to stay alive. He dodged frantically to the right, up through the brush laid low by the charge of buckshot. A revolver crashed behind him, and he knew Pete Shatto had joined in. He heard the deadly whistle of the projectile rake the spot where he had been but an instant before.

He was running, hunched over. His own gun roared as the man with the shotgun flung the empty weapon aside and brought up a revolver. He never had a chance to use it, for Kirk's shot tore away the left side of the face. The man dropped loosely into the dust and didn't move.

Still running, Kirk managed to outguess Shatto, who was firing blindly at his back. Kirk could hear the bullets slam into aspen trunks beyond the shack. He reached the first trees and took two steps to the right and whirled. The maneuver threw Shatto off and his shot was wide. Kirk saw Pete Shatto standing with thin legs braced, drawing back the hammer of his revolver for another frenzied shot.

Because he wanted the man alive, Kirk tried for the legs. But Shatto, moving toward his mule, stumbled at that moment. He took the bullet in the chest. It knocked him sprawling. Stunned by the suddenness of the attack, which had consumed no more than a dozen heartbeats, Kirk stood for a shaky moment, his revolver an unaccustomed weight in his right hand. The silence after the roar of gunfire was almost deafening. He looked around at the three crumpled figures. His mouth was dry. His heart was a sledge blow in his ears.

The mountains rose purple against the sky. A hawk's wing cut blackly against the face of a cliff. The mule brayed off in the brush.

He stumbled toward Pete Shatto, whose long dirty fingers clawed at the dust. Kirk turned him over, got his gun, and flung it into the brush. Shatto's eyes were dull with shock.

"You write me to meet you, then set up a trap," Kirk said. "Why, Pete?"

Shatto was bleeding at the mouth, and his breath was ragged, as if he had run a great distance. "Both ends against the middle—I tried to play it that way. Is—is Charlie dead?"

"The one with the shotgun? Yeah, he's dead."

"My brother," Shatto gasped, and closed his eyes. "You alone we could've handled. But when Dunster come. I wanted to figure a new plan, but Dunster got tough with me and—" His mouth hung open.

"Walt Chance paid you to gun us down."

"I—I said you wrote that you was comin' here, and I was to get a thousand dollars if you was buried here."

"Walt gave you a thousand dollars to bury me?"

"Wait, you got to listen to me," Shatto said. His face was gray.

Kirk was on his knees beside the man. "Where is Walt, damn it? Tell me, Pete. You'll die easier."

Shatto's lips were pulled away from his teeth. There was blood on them. "I ain't dyin' easy, Fallon." He gestured feebly toward the mule. "Bottle in saddlebag—gimme drink. . . ."

When Kirk returned with the bottle, Shatto was dead.

Kirk put a shaking hand across his forehead. Only because of the inexperience of the two ambushers was he alive. He stared at the clouds torn by the wind against the high peaks of the Cobres. The sun was warm on the back of his neck. A haze of gunsmoke lay across the clearing.

He went through Shatto's pockets, finding only an overdue bill for harness at the Giant Store in El Cobre, and two silver dollars.

"I'll find Walt Chance," he vowed grimly. "I'll find him if it takes twenty years."

He got to his feet and stiffened when he saw an auburn-haired girl slipping downwind from the horses to the edge of the shack. She held a rifle in slim brown hands. As she advanced, her bosom stirred under a plaid shirt. She wore Levis and scuffed boots. Her hair was in braids.

"Robbing the dead," she said in a husky voice. "This is getting to be a fine country. Mighty fine."

"No," he said, and kept his hand away from his gun.

"You were going through his pockets."

"I thought maybe Shatto carried something that would tell me where I could find a man named Walt Chance."

She came forward, watching him out of narrowed green eyes. He told her about Chance and the gun trap and how Dunster had been caught in it.

"There's nobody around here named Chance," she said.

"He's probably changed his name," Kirk said. "He doesn't change his face. I'll find him."

She was studying him, as if trying to make up her mind. "I heard shooting when I was up on the ridge. I saw Charlie Shatto with the shotgun and Pete at your back." She shook her auburn head. "Mister, you're lucky."

"I shot to save my own neck. I'll tell my story to the law."

"The law?" She laughed bitterly. "We've heard of it. We haven't seen much in these parts, though."

Curiosity edged her toward Dunster's body, sprawled at the edge of the clearing. She got her first close look at the damage done by the shotgun at close range. Her face went white and her knees sagged. In one bound Kirk reached her and tore the rifle away. Holding her with one hand, he avoided her fingernails. After a moment she relaxed. A braid of auburn hair had fallen across her tanned throat. Her hair smelled of wood smoke.

He told her he had no intention of hurting her, and put the rifle on the ground.

Her green eyes softened. She turned her back and adjusted her shirt, which had come unbuttoned during the brief struggle.

When she faced around again she gave him a tight smile. "Sometimes I think I'm a man. Then I see something like that"—she flung out a hand toward Dunster's body—"and I go all weak in the knees."

"If there's no law hereabouts, what'll I do with the bodies?"

"Do what you want with your friend," she said, her

face still pale from the shock of seeing Dunster. "I never had much use for the Shatto brothers, but I feel sorry for Irma." She looked at Pete Shatto, lying with his knees drawn up, his mouth open. "I'll take you down to Larnet's Store. Pete and Charlie belonged to the pool. I'll tell the boys how it happened."

While she went to get the horse she had left in the trees, he scooped out a grave for Ard Dunster. Steeling himself, he went through the man's pockets. He found $285 in a leather sack. Kirk knew from his talks with Danny Dunster so long ago in Mexico that the brothers had no kin.

Kirk covered Dunster's grave and licked a drop of sweat from his upper lip.

With Pete Shatto's body lashed to a mule, his brother's to a chestnut horse, Kirk let the girl lead him to Larnet's Store, where the Juniper Pool hung out. Her name was Libby Squires and she owned a small spread in the mountains. She belonged to the pool.

"I've got a feeling about you, Fallon," she said. "I think your coming here is somehow going to blow this country wide open."

They reached the road and continued north. They saw a great cloud of dust and heard a clacking of wheels and hoofs. Soon they saw a stage toiling up the grade, and because of the narrow road, Kirk pulled off. When the driver saw the mule and the chestnut with the two bodies tied on, he brought the stagecoach to a halt.

"What in hell's goin' on, Libby?" he demanded of the girl.

"Our friend here," she said, indicating Fallon, "killed the Shatto brothers."

The driver, a small whip-lean man with a sparse gray beard, gave Kirk a startled look. "By damn," he breathed. "Looks like Beartrack's done hired a gun hand to clean out the pool. You better watch out, Libby."

The stagecoach door opened abruptly and a tall, black-haired girl stepped out. She glared at Kirk, then looked up at the driver, her mouth white. "Beartrack has never hired gunmen!" she said in a rich deep voice that trembled in anger. "It never will."

The driver's mouth opened. "'Scuse me, Miss Berryman. I plumb forgot you're aboard."

She wheeled and faced Kirk, her long dark eyes studying his tall, dusty figure. Her eyes rested on the cedar-handled gun, then lifted again to his face

"If these were my Beartrack men you'd killed," she said thinly, indicating the bodies with a sweep of a strong hand, "you'd hang for it."

Libby Squires swung down. The coach team, smelling blood, stirred restlessly. "Kirk Fallon killed the Shatto brothers in self-defense," she said, and from the way the two women glared at each other, Kirk had the feeling that theirs was an old enmity. "I saw the whole thing from the ridge," Libby went on.

"I'd hardly take the word of a woman like you," the Berryman girl said crisply. She wore a bonnet on her blue-black hair, and a light traveling cloak, which she had thrown open because of the heat. Kirk could see the thrust of a young bosom against China silk.

A moon-faced Indian woman leaned out the coach window. "Señorita, if we do not hurry we will not reach Junction in time for the stage to Santa Fe."

The Berryman girl seemed not to hear. There was a paleness around the full mouth that cut beautifully across the lower half of her face. Kirk had faced tough men in the war and on the frontier, but facing this girl was not an easy thing to do. Because of his work he had sometimes been hated. But never before had anyone looked at him with such revulsion.

"A common killer," she said. "That's the trouble with this country. Too many men like you who'd rather shoot than talk."

A fat drummer wearing a wrinkled brown suit stepped out of the coach and took a look at the bodies. They were an ugly sight, lashed to the horse and mule; green flies were clusters of live color against the wounds.

"You're Kirk Fallon," the fat man said. "Sure, I recollect you from Dodge City and Borden. You come over this way to do some lawin' for the folks?"

"I'm over here looking for a man. Walt Chance. Any of you know him?"

The girl took a backward step, her mouth loose.

The driver said from the high seat, "Never heard of anybody named Chance."

"Me neither," the fat drummer said.

"He paid the Shatto brothers to set up a gun trap," Kirk said coldly. "When I find him I think I'll kill him."

The girl put a hand to the coach door to steady herself. The driver was having a time holding in the nervous six-horse team.

Kirk swung down, trailed the reins, and took a step toward the girl. "This name Walt Chance means something to you," he stated.

She drew back as if having him that close were the most revolting thing that had ever happened to her. She was about twenty, a year one way or the other, maybe. Younger than Libby Squires. Her face was dead white.

"You're upset," Kirk told her, watching the dark eyes. They were shining with a sort of unholy fear.

"It's the heat," she said, and turned for the coach. The drummer offered his hand, then climbed in himself. The driver kicked off the brake and the horses lunged into their collars. The coach moved slowly up the grade, a great cloud of yellow dust curling through the aspens in its wake.

Kirk said, "Did you see how she acted when I mentioned Walt Chance?"

Libby Squires was staring after the coach, her eyes bitter. "I'm surprised the great lady could show that much feeling about anything," she said with a trace of venom in her voice.

As they continued on toward Larnet's Store, Kirk asked Libby about the Berryman girl. Her name was Vanessa. Two years before, her father had bought Beartrack, down on the flats, and she had come out from St. Louis to live with him. Because of the trouble here between Beartrack and the Juniper Pool, the girl was going to Santa Fe to visit a woman friend of her late mother's.

"What's her father look like?" Kirk asked.

"Gray hair. Mustache. Shorter than you."

Kirk frowned, thinking, In five years black hair can turn to gray.

Libby said, "Berryman isn't much of a man. The whole country laughs behind his back. Rex Havenrite used to be one of us up here, but he threw in his Cross Box with Beartrack so they could have water. It's been a dry year in more ways than one." Libby's shoulders shrugged under the faded boy's shirt. "When she gets back from Santa Fe she'll marry Havenrite."

"That's one way for a man to get a ranch. Marry it."

"Don't think Rex hasn't laid awake nights planning

it. Rex and his old man came here about the same time my folks did. The country used to make fun of Old Man Havenrite because he'd shovel manure for the price of a bottle. But nobody laughs at Rex. He's out to prove he's the biggest man in this country. He might just do it, too."

"You don't like him," Kirk said.

She looked at him out of her green eyes. "A long time ago I was in love with Rex. I was younger then. I didn't know much about ambitious men. But I learned."

Chapter Three

It was full dark when they reached Larnet's Store, set in a clearing back from the road. It was a one-story log building. Some men were on the porch, and when they saw Libby and the stranger with the mule and the chestnut horse, they picked up rifles and came to the yard. There was a tense watchfulness about these heavily armed men.

When the bodies were cut loose, Kirk put his back to the store wall, a hand on his gun, while Libby told her story. Some of the men, cursing and muttering threats, looked from the two dead brothers to Kirk. A short bald man wearing steel-rimmed spectacles seemed to be in charge. He was Ray Larnet. When Libby finished telling how she had observed the shooting from the ridge while she was hunting strays, there was a moment of silence.

"Kirk Fallon, eh?" Larnet mused, turning his pinched-in storekeeper's face on the new arrival. "Pete got drunk in my place last week. He said you were coming here and it would make him some easy money. Pete was such a liar that I didn't pay much attention. Anyhow, they killed Ard Dunster, and that's something. I've heard of that son, and there was nothing good about what I heard."

Kirk said, "No matter what he was, Ard didn't deserve to die with no hope of defending himself."

There was the sound of horses off in the trees and the men faced that way, lifting their rifles.

"Hold it, boys," Larnet warned. "It's only Purley and Yáñez. Libby, here comes the light of your life."

Libby said, "Quit it, Ray," and, glancing at Kirk, added, "Jed's only a neighbor."

Kirk read something in the girl's green eyes that sent a faint stirring along his spine. She wanted him to know she was unattached. But he had other things on his mind. It wasn't the first time in five years a pretty woman had tried to get him to turn casual attraction into something permanent. He imagined a man could become pretty attached to someone like Libby. But he wasn't having any. He still had Walt Chance to find.

"He's hunting for somebody named Walt Chance," Libby explained when the two newcomers had come up. "Have any of you heard the name?"

Nobody had. Jed Purley was thick in the neck and the shoulders. When Libby told her story of the shooting again, Kirk felt his first antagonism. Not from the slender, smiling Mexican, Ramón Yáñez. But from Purley. And Purley seemed to dislike the fact that Kirk and Libby had been off in the back country together. Even if their mission had been the grisly one of bringing two dead men here to the store.

"How we know Fallon ain't been hired by Rex Havenrite?" Purley demanded. A lock of coarse brown hair angled across his low forehead.

Libby said, "Don't worry about that." She told them how Vanessa Berryman had reacted when the stage driver had voiced the same opinion.

"Don't prove nothin'," Purley rumbled. There was a not-too-bright look in his pale eyes. "Havenrite runs Beartrack to suit himself. If he hired Fallon, the girl wouldn't know nothin' about it. Besides, she's spending six months in Santa Fe, so I hear."

Ray Larnet said, "We called a meeting tonight, not to wonder about Fallon, but to discuss Beartrack. The fact that the Shatto brothers got themselves killed is incidental. How many cows did you boys lose this time?"

This brought on a chorus of angry voices. The men cursed Beartrack in the big store with its odors of gun oil and coffee and leather. There was a long counter that took up one wall, and above it shelves of tinned goods and coils of rope and saddles. There was a big Beal and Harper stove for winter warmth. Across the back of the store was a short bar. Here Larnet served whisky in tin cups. The men sat around and grimly discussed their cattle losses.

Beartrack had put the knife in them and was now twisting it. Six months ago Beartrack had managed to get the contract to deliver beef to Fort Bedloe to feed the Apaches. The contract had formerly been held by the dozen Juniper Pool members. That was the knife. The twisting of it concerned the pool cattle Beartrack had picked up on the drives to the fort.

Old Man Hoskins, gray-bearded, with a thin, bitter mouth, said, "I lost forty-two head this time." His two gangling, hard-eyed sons, stood on either side, rifle butts resting beside their big feet.

The other pool members had lost cattle.

Kirk said, "If the Army has a contract for Beartrack cattle, how come they'll accept beef in other brands?"

Ray Larnet shook his head. "The major at the fort is money-hungry. He'll buy cattle and to hell with brands. Just so he gets his cut of the beef."

Kirk listened to them discuss their problem. He had his own problem. The fast trip from Kansas had ground the weariness into his very bones. He needed a shave and a change of clothing. He ate the meat sandwiches Larnet made up for him, and contemplated how best to continue his search for Walt Chance.

In his pocket he carried a statement he had prepared for presentation to Chance:

Two bullet wounds at $500 each....$1,000
Three months laid up.............. 1,000
My share of horse herd............ 5,000
My share of savings you stole....... 800
Total owed Kirk Fallon by Walt
Chance $7,800

Larnet was talking to Jed Purley. "Did Havenrite go with the herd this time to Fort Bedloe?"

Purley shook his head. "He sent Bob Coleman." Kirk had gathered that Coleman was the Beartrack *segundo*. "Coleman is goin' to bring back the money for the herd." Purley looked around at the tense faces.

Yáñez said, "So we take the money. How many of you ride with us?"

There was a moment of silence as the men shifted their feet nervously. Kirk smiled to himself. It was an old familiar story, these ranchers with a patch on a patch trying to make out in what was becoming increasingly a rich man's business. They were long on talk, but short on action.

Yáñez tipped back his high-peaked hat. "Then Jed and me go alone, no?"

"No," Libby said, getting to her feet from the cracker barrel where she had been sitting. "It's a fool play."

"They've stole their last cow of mine," Purley said.

The silence deepened. Tobacco smoke drifted toward the rafters. Outside the horses stirred. In the wavering light of kerosene lamps the faces of these men reflected the years of hard work, disappointment, hopelessness. Only Purley and the Mexican seemed intent on doing anything. Purley ranched the sections north of Libby's place. Yáñez ran a few head of cattle near the rim where Old Man Hoskins and his two sons had the most pretentious mountain layout.

Libby faced Purley. "I'll repeat what I said the other night." She clenched her fists. "Don't take a gun. It's what Havenrite wants. You do that and you're not my friend."

Purley scowled as his slow brain tried to digest the threat. Purley took a step toward her, lifting his big hands, trying to get her to understand. When he was near her he seemed to lose his bull voice. "Listen, Libby, I—"

She cut him off. "Remember what I said, Jed."

Purley took a hitch at his gunbelt and put a thick arm about Libby's waist. "You let me play this game my way," he said, and tried to grin. "Keep the coffee hot for me." He looked across the store at Kirk Fallon. "Me and Libby figure to get married one of these days."

Purley and Yáñez started for the door. Purley swung around. "There ain't nobody named Walt Chance in these parts, Fallon. Reckon Pete Shatto pulled a long bow on you. You better head somewheres else to look for your man."

Kirk cast a tall shadow across the rough plank flooring. "I'll look where I feel like it, Purley," he said.

Purley started for him, but Yáñez caught him by an arm and whispered something. Purley relaxed and followed the Mexican outside. In a moment there was the sound of two horses moving off.

Old Man Hoskins straightened his lank frame away from the wall. "You boys might as well know that Beartrack's made me an offer for my place. If you let Purley do some damn-fool thing, I—"

"You going to let Havenrite and Berryman sleep under your blankets?" Larnet asked thinly.

"I like my spread," Hoskins said, coloring under the

storekeeper's sarcasm. "But I don't figure to be buried up there."

He went out, his two big sons slouching along with their rifles.

Libby said, "Somebody will have to tell Pete Shatto's widow." She looked at Kirk. "Might be decent if you rode up with me to explain."

"Explaining to a woman why I killed her husband isn't easy," he said.

She watched him a moment. "I'll go and tell her alone. I guess it's a lot to ask of a man."

He gave her a hard look, searching the green eyes, the red mouth. There was a narrow-lidded boldness about her.

He gave her the money he had taken from Ard Dunster, and made up the rest of the $500 reward from his own money belt. "Give this to Shatto's widow," he said, putting the gold coins in neat stacks on the bar. "It's what I promised Pete. And I guess he earned it, in a way, because he's brought me close to Walt Chance."

The pool members crowded around, staring at the coins. It was a lot of money to men who ran scrawny cattle and were lucky to pay up their bill at Larnet's Store at the end of the year.

Libby put the coins in a sack. "Irma would sell the ranch cheap," Libby said. "She always hated it. You could do worse, Fallon." She looked at him hopefully.

"I haven't settled down in five years. I don't intend to now. Not until I find Chance."

He went to the porch and stood in the darkness, looking at the two forms under a tarp. Had it not been for sheer luck, he would now be as dead as the Shatto brothers.

Libby came to stand beside him, looking at the stars above the high ridges.

"Do you know what a Chihuahua saddle looks like?" he asked her.

"Sure. It's made of hackberry mesquite and has an oversize horn." She looked at him curiously. "Why?"

"Walt Chance had a fondness for Mexican saddles," Kirk said.

She stood plucking at one of the thick braids of her hair. "Sam Berryman rode a Chihuahua saddle when he first came here. Maybe he still does, for all I know."

"But Berryman's got a daughter," Kirk said, "and if Chance had one, it's funny he never mentioned it."

"Some men keep lots of things hidden in closets. Why not a daughter?"

"Doesn't seem that a man like Walt Chance could sire a beauty like Vanessa Berryman."

Libby turned to stare up at his face, hard now in the wash of light from the store. "If Berryman should turn out to be Walt Chance," Libby said seriously, "you've got as much chance of fighting him as you have the U.S. Army."

He went down the steps to his horse. He jerked a thumb at Dunster's black horse, tied at the rail. "Maybe Irma Shatto can use an extra mount. It's hers if she wants it." In the saddle he lifted a hand to her. She seemed small and somehow defenseless at the moment, standing on the porch in the darkness. She was a woman in a tough man's country, fighting a man's tough fight. "I hope you folks up here win your battle."

"I'd like to believe that you'll win yours," she said, "but I don't."

He rode down out of the mountains toward the town of El Cobre.

Chapter Four

VANESSA BERRYMAN'S sudden return to El Cobre on the morning stage was the cause of much speculation among the townspeople. But she offered no explanation as to why she had not continued her trip to Santa Fe. She had been driven in a rented buggy through the hills to Beartrack.

When they topped the rise above the sprawling building of Beartrack headquarters, Vanessa caught her breath. The view never lost its fascination. The buildings were of stone, with narrow windows for strategic reasons; the ranch had been founded during the Indian trouble. Poplars and junipers formed a windbreak around the main house with its white fence and carved stone lions that guarded the curving drive. The place had been founded by an Englishman named Beshears, with more money than a savvy of ranching.

There had been enough trouble at Beartrack during the two years of the Berryman ownership, but now there was a new threat. She intended to meet it, not as her father would, but head on.

She found her father in the room in the west wing of the house that he used for an office. When he saw her his mouth fell open and it took him a moment to recover.

"I thought you'd be halfway to Santa Fe by this time," he said, and pulled a chair around for her. "What brings you back, honey?" He looked worried.

She sat rigidly in the slat-seat chair and slipped the dusty traveling cloak from her shoulders.

He seemed frail and so much grayer than he had two years ago, when he had come to St. Louis and told her of this wonderful opportunity to own a ranch. Such a beautiful place, he said. And it was. She loved it. But she had known even less about the cattle business than her father. She had not realized that without water . . .

"Dad, did you ever know a man named Fallon, Kirk Fallon?"

Berryman frowned, picked up some papers on his desk, and made a great show of stacking them neatly. "Kirk Fallon," he repeated. "He used to be my partner. Why do you ask?"

She told him about the tall, rough-looking man in the mountains who had killed the Shatto brothers.

Berryman looked puzzled. With a nervous hand he smoothed his thick down-curving gray mustache. His hands were small, well shaped. "Kirk Fallon is dead," Berryman said.

"Then it's somebody using his name," the girl said, watching this father she hardly knew. "But I doubt it."

"No, it couldn't be," Berryman said weakly. "Kirk's dead. I saw him die." Berryman forced a smile. "Now you rest up for a day or so and then take the stage to Santa Fe."

"I've changed my mind. I'm not going."

"But—there may be trouble here. I don't want you to see anything ugly."

"I own a majority of the stock in Beartrack," she reminded him. "It's my place to stay here and not run when things go against us." When she saw the hurt in his eyes she felt contrite, for she knew it had hit home. She had not meant to be so blunt. Sam Berryman was a man who ran easily when there was unpleasantness to face.

She tried to soften it. "Dad, I just don't want to see you hurt," she explained. "That's why I came home instead of going to Santa Fe."

Berryman licked at a thin underlip. "Did this man calling himself Kirk Fallon mention my name?"

"The name you used in Mexico, Dad," she said, and saw a flush on his cheek. "Walt Chance."

He put a hand on the desk to steady the trembling in his body. "How did you know that name?"

"When mother died I went through some old letters," Vanessa said. "They were from Chihuahua, Mexico. You told her that down there you were known as Walt Chance, and if she wanted to write she was to address you by that name. You said that someday you'd explain."

Sam Berryman seemed to have aged in the few minutes they had been talking. There was a murmur of voices from the back part of the house as the Mexican servants went about their chores. A cowboy in the yard shouted at a balky horse.

"I thought it was all done and forgotten," Sam Berryman said. "Now it's come back to kick me in the face."

"I'm on your side, Dad," she said. "We'll fight this Kirk Fallon together."

When his daughter had gone to her room, Sam Berryman removed a bottle from a drawer of his desk. For several minutes he sat staring at the amber-colored liquid, as if trying to make up his mind. Then he uncorked the bottle and killed half of the contents before he went out into the yard.

His gait was unsteady as he walked through the aspens and down the long yard, past the corrals and the barns and the outbuildings. Some punchers in front of the blacksmith shop grinned at Berryman's back and mimicked his dignified drunken walk.

He passed the bunkhouse and then the quarters for the married riders. A brown-haired homely woman was nursing a baby in front of one of the doors.

"Mornin', Mrs. Oldcamp," Berryman said, and tried not to look at the breast clutched by the eager infant. He wondered then, as he continued on his way, if the baby would grow up to be a shiftless fifty-dollar-a-month cow hand like its father, Si Oldcamp.

He found Havenrite just dismounting in front of the quarters formerly used by the Beartrack foreman. When Havenrite had consolidated his mountain ranch with Beartrack, he had been given a 25-per-cent interest in the big spread. The foreman had been fired. Havenrite acted as his own foreman.

"I got a trap baited for the Juniper Pool bunch," Havenrite said, showing his large even teeth in a grin. "I hope to hell they bite on it."

Berryman followed him into the small room. It had a cot, desk, and big iron safe. Berryman sank to the cot. "Vanessa didn't go to Santa Fe," he said, and explained how she had returned that morning.

Havenrite's amber gaze was thoughtful. He wore a striped wool shirt and black pants. His shell belt was heavy with silverwork. His gun was bone-handled. A big man, two inches over six feet. There was a handsome, reckless look about him.

"Now that she's home," Berryman said, "you better go easy on your plan to drive that mountain bunch off their grass."

Havenrite sniffed the air. "You've been at that bottle again," he said. "You better quit it, Sam. You can't handle it."

Berryman flushed. He glared at the big man who one day would be his son-in-law.

"You don't like me very much, do you, Sam?" Havenrite said.

Berryman stiffened, not liking to face Havenrite's wrath. But how could you like or trust a man who would turn against his former friends in the mountains? And plan to hang or shoot those he could not intimidate?

Havenrite seemed to read his mind. "Remember this, Sam," the big man said bluntly. "I come in here and saved Beartrack. If it wasn't for me, old Bert Wingate would've picked up the ranch for ten cents on the dollar and added it to his Six Bar. And you and your daughter would be begging stagecoach tickets to get you out of town."

"I appreciate all you've done, Rex," Berryman said, wilting. "But I wish we could be satisfied with what we have."

"The East wants beef and we're going to give it to them," Havenrite said, his amber eyes lighted with the hard shine of ambition. "I'm dickering for a beef contract that'll make this Fort Bedloe deal look like old-maid poker. But we need more water, more graze. That crazy Englishman who laid this place out figured to graze fifty cows to the section. He was a millionaire, but he damn near went under tryin' to buy hay to feed those cows." He regarded Berryman sharply. "You got something else on your mind, Sam?"

Berryman hesitated a moment, then told him about Kirk Fallon.

Havenrite listened, lit a cigar, then rested a hand on Berryman's thin shoulder. "Sam, when I took over here I said you wouldn't have to worry any more. I meant it."

Berryman moved away from the hand on his shoulder. "If this really is Fallon—and it can't be possible—the problem won't be easily solved."

Havenrite dug a letter from a desk drawer and handed it over. "Pete Shatto left this for you at Oberley's Saloon. I told Oberley I'd give it to you. But I got curious as hell about what that sick-eyed cowman wanted with you." He flicked a long forefinger at the letter Berryman held in his shaking hands. "Read it, Sam."

Berryman began to read and his face lost even more color.

Dear Mr. Berryman:

Kirk Fallon, who is marshal at Borden, Kansas, and a tough man like you remember from Mexico, is going to pay me $500 if I show you to him. I was thinking that since you and me are neighbors here, me and my brother would see that we done a neighborly thing and saw to it that Fallon don't find you. You think Fallon's dead, but he ain't. And he aims to kill you more than likely. My brother and me would like $1,000 for keeping Fallon from shooting you. Let me know about it.

Your neighbor,
PETE SHATTO

Berryman sat as if frozen.

"I beat the hell out of Pete Shatto," Havenrite said, and cracked heavy knuckles. "I told him to get that Fallon out here and bury him in the Cobres. I said I'd pay him the thousand dollars if he did that." Havenrite chuckled. "I said he'd have a thousand from Beartrack and the five hundred Fallon would be bringing. Shatto's eyes nearly jumped out of his head at the idea of all that money."

Berryman let the letter fall to the floor from his lifeless fingers.

Havenrite said, "I never figured to pay Shatto. He don't know it, but he's working for nothing." Havenrite regarded the man for a long moment. "According to a letter Shatto got from Fallon, you're supposed to have killed a fella named Danny Dunster and shot Fallon."

"No!" Berryman cried, springing to his feet. "It was the Comanches that did it. I couldn't kill a man, Rex."

Havenrite chewed his cigar. "Tell you what, Sam. You talk Vanessa into taking that trip to Santa Fe, and you go with her."

Berryman shook his head. "I'm safer here."

Havenrite gave a harsh laugh. "You scared of this Fallon?"

"He killed the Shatto brothers."

Havenrite scowled and rubbed his heavy jaw. "Well, that's two less pool members to worry about, anyhow. Tell Vanessa I'll be up for supper tonight."

When Berryman had gone, Havenrite said under his breath, "No guts. No guts at all."

At the Fort Bedloe Junction, twelve miles east of the Rim Pass through the Cobre Mountains, Jed Purley and Yáñez smoked cigarillos and watched the road. They were on a bluff screened by buckbrush. In the clear air they could see the haze of smoke that marked the site of the fort, twenty miles north. Now they got to their knees, eyes watching an approaching column of dust.

Yáñez threw aside his cigarillo and picked up his rifle. "Here they come," he said, and started for his horse, tied off in the brush.

Jed Purley's narrow forehead wrinkled as he tried to analyze the situation. "There's only three of 'em," he said dubiously. "How come Havenrite didn't send more than that?"

Yáñez was already in the saddle. "It is lucky for us, no?"

On the road Bob Coleman, *segundo* for Beartrack, rode with black-bearded Hank Ogden and the lazy tobacco-chewing Si Oldcamp. Ogden, a stocky man who trimmed his own beard with a belt knife, was telling about a girl he had met once in Austin.

Coleman wasn't listening. He was a slightly built, sandy-haired man. In a day of drifters he had an intense loyalty toward any man who paid his salary, whether he liked that man or not. In his saddlebags was the three thousand dollars Beartrack had been paid for the cattle they had delivered to the fort.

He was trying to make sense out of Havenrite's orders. Havenrite had ordered eight of the eleven men making the drive to cut north and look for strays over in the Snake Creek area. Bob Coleman was to come straight back to Beartrack with the money, using only Ogden and Oldcamp as guards.

He had no time to dwell on the matter further. As they entered a canyon they suddenly saw two riders at a bend in the road. Coleman pulled up and said under his breath to his companions, "There's that ox-headed Purley. Watch it, boys."

Purley and Yáñez urged their horses forward. Both men held rifles.

Coleman's face turned red. "What's the idea?"

"The money," Jed Purley said. He was big, a sweat-soaked bandanna knotted about his thick neck.

Coleman stiffened in the saddle. "The hell with you," he said.

Purley showed his teeth. "Beartrack stole our cows. We're collecting."

Coleman flushed. "I got orders to take the money to Beartrack. That's what I'm doin'. You can argue the cow business with Havenrite or Berryman."

Yáñez laughed pleasantly but did not lower his rifle. "This Berryman would not know a cow from a burro."

Hank Ogden carefully lifted a hand to his black beard and said, "Better let 'em have the money, Bob."

"Yeah," Si Oldcamp put in. "Ain't no use arguing with a rifle."

Coleman turned and gave the two riders a look of disgust. "Who's side you on, anyhow?"

"We just don't hanker to get shot up," Ogden said. "It ain't no hair off your head if Beartrack loses money."

Coleman turned in his saddle. It was hot in the canyon. The horses switched tails at bottle-green flies. Squirrels chattered from a nest of rocks.

"You won't get away with this," Coleman told Purley and Yáñez. Then he made as if to swing down. Instead he reached for his revolver, jabbing in spurs at the same moment.

As his horse lunged, spooking the mounts of Ogden and Oldcamp, a rifle crashed. Coleman was dumped from the saddle. He lay on his back in the road dust. A wisp of smoke was torn by the breeze from the muzzle of Yáñez' rifle.

Ogden and Oldcamp had right hands in the air, while they fought their horses to a standstill with their left hands on the reins.

"That was a damn-fool play, Bob," Purley said, and looked worried. "We had you covered."

Coleman's left shoulder was bleeding. The man stared up at them dazedly.

Yáñez said, "I think it is best if we hurry." He glanced

anxiously down the road. There was no sound of approaching riders, no indication that any hunter or cow hand might have heard the shot and intended to investigate.

"Bob should've had more sense," Hank Ogden said. Then he added, "The money's in his saddlebags."

Chapter Five

KIRK FALLON had spent the day in El Cobre. Now it was early evening. Charcoal cook fires laid their blue-gray smudge over the flat roofs. Shadows fell upon the cracked adobe walls and the false fronts of the single business block. The ancestors of the Mexicans lounging in the plaza had mined copper here and given the town its name. Then the village had slept for a hundred years, until the *yanquis* found a future here in the raising of cattle.

Kirk got his horse from the Atlas Livery and tied it in the alley beside Oberley's Saloon. He intended to have a drink or two, eat his supper, and then do some scouting in the direction of Beartrack. He had taken a room at the Lee House, across the street, bought a new shirt, shaved and bathed at the barbershop at the end of the block.

Oberley's was a flat-roofed adobe structure with a low ceiling. There were a few men at the bar, gossiping, spitting, scuffing their spurs into the oiled dirt floor. Other men were watching a two-handed poker game at a rear table.

When Kirk entered and looked around, the men glanced up and there was a nudging of elbows in ribs. With no expression on his tight brown face, he walked to the bar and ordered a drink. He knew his arrival in El Cobre was the cause of much speculation.

Oberley, a rangy man with sparse hair parted in the center of a high-domed skull, set out a bottle for Kirk. Then he moved unobtrusively to a rear poker table and said something to one of the players in the two-handed poker game. The man listened to Oberley, then put his amber eyes the length of the barroom to rest on the tall man just pouring himself a drink.

"I've had enough, Bert," Havenrite told the other player. "Your luck's too good."

Bert Wingate was small-boned, but tough-looking in an expensive brown suit. He raked in some chips and cast a glance at the yellow-haired man at the bar. Wingate, in his middle fifties, owned the 6 Bar west of El Cobre.

"Don't get a cat by the tail," Wingate told Havenrite. "That boy looks tough."

Havenrite laughed and got to his feet and moved down the baroom. His shoulders were wide, his arms heavy. His wool shirt did not hide the depth of his chest. As he moved, the harness holding his bone-handled gun gave off a dry leather creaking.

"They tell me you been looking for somebody named Walt Chance," Havenrite said in his heavy voice.

Kirk nodded. He had seen Havenrite ride in earlier on a Beartrack-branded horse. The arrogant way he sat his saddle, the purposeful way he walked stamped him as a man of ambition.

"You asked a lot of questions around town," Havenrite said. "We don't like strangers who ask questions."

A faint smile touched Kirk's mouth. "The only way to learn is to ask." He moved away from the bar so his right arm would not be pinned against it.

There was a tense quiet in the barroom. A man turned his chair noisily. Bert Wingate narrowly watched Kirk and Havenrite from the poker table.

Havenrite said, "Your name Fallon?"

"Yes."

"Some people seem to think you died in Mexico."

"Do I look dead?"

A hard light leaped into the amber eyes. "Not right now you don't look dead," Havenrite said. "But you never can tell."

Kirk felt the tension in his right arm. He thought of the tough ones he had seen in his years as marshal or deputy or gun guard. The whiners, the crazy killers. But this Havenrite was smart and wouldn't be goaded into making a move unless he was sure of having the upper hand. And he had it now. The saloon was obviously packed with his friends, or at least with men who would keep out of any trouble because of their fear.

"I hear you met up with the Shatto brothers," Havenrite said.

"Yeah," Kirk said. "They had a trap rigged. It didn't work. Who put them up to it?"

Havenrite shrugged his heavy shoulders. "Nobody will miss the Shatto brothers, so you're clear there, Fallon. But if I were you, I'd drift. Next time you might shoot the wrong man. We've buried a few tough ones in this town. We haven't forgotten how."

Kirk's yellow brows were level across his eyes. "It took five years and a lot of miles to get here. I'll leave when I finish my business." He added, "If I'm buried here, I'll have company."

The silence deepened. A man coughed. Oberley, behind his bar, looked frightened. "Let's not wreck the place, boys," he said nervously.

Neither man paid any attention. Havenrite's mouth showed pressure. Kirk stood tall, hands at his sides. The cedar-butted gun he wore showed care. The holster was trimmed a little for a faster draw. It was thonged to his leg. Havenrite was letting his amber eyes study the gun.

Kirk said, "You know about Walt Chance. How about taking me to him?"

Havenrite said, "Sure."

"But we'll go alone—to Beartrack. It's Sam Berryman, isn't it?"

"Yeah, it is."

Kirk sighed. He was glad the Berryman girl was on her way to Santa Fe and would not have to witness the ugly business that would inevitably follow.

"Let's go," Kirk said.

Havenrite smiled thinly and half turned as if to head for the door. Then he swung around and struck Kirk on the side of the head with a heavy fist. The tremendous power of the blow drove Kirk to his knees. But before Havenrite could close in, Kirk lunged at the man. He hit him with a shoulder just above the knees. Havenrite crashed into one of the poker tables, upsetting it.

Kirk got to his feet, waiting. Havenrite was on the floor, shaking his head. He had struck his forehead on a corner of the table and was blinking his eyes and trying to push himself up.

The men waited, watching tensely.

"Don't tear things up, boys," Oberley was pleading. "Take your fight into the street."

Havenrite got to his feet and said, "Shut up, Ed."

Before he could advance on Kirk there was a sudden clatter of hoofs in front of the saloon. A moment later the stocky black-bearded Hank Ogden rushed in, shouting, "Havenrite! Bob Coleman's been shot."

Havenrite picked up his hat from the floor. "Who shot him, Hank?"

Hank Ogden said loudly for everyone's benefit, "The pool. Who else? Somebody better get the doc."

Havenrite started for the door, then looked back at Kirk. "Too bad this had to happen," he said thinly. "I'd enjoy knocking down Oberley's bar with the back of your head."

Then, followed by Hank Ogden, he went out where a crowd was gathered about the wounded Beartrack *segundo*. Si Oldcamp was excitedly telling how the man had been shot.

"And Purley and Yáñez got away with three thousand dollars," Oldcamp finished.

"I warned 'em," Havenrite said, shaking his fist at the darkening sky. "I told 'em if they hit Beartrack I'd stretch some necks."

Bert Wingate had come to the saloon porch. "You better go easy with this business, Rex," the 6 Bar owner advised grimly.

But Havenrite ignored him. He gestured to Oldcamp and the bearded Ogden. "Come on, boys, we're going to have some fine hunting tonight."

There was an ominous silence in the street as the three Beartrack men thundered away on their horses.

Bert Wingate said sourly, "A damn range war, that's what we'll have. Widows will be counting their dead before this is over."

Kirk stood on the porch, looking through the saloon window while a fat little man with mutton-chop whiskers bandaged Bob Coleman's wounded shoulder. Coleman seemed shaken and bitter.

And Kirk had his own bitterness. At last he knew the name Walt Chance had been hiding under. No wonder he had never been able to find the man. He moved along the almost deserted street. Everyone was in the saloon or crowded in the street outside, discussing the possibility of a savage fight to the finish between Beartrack and the Juniper Pool.

He passed the plaza, listening to a woman sing softly in Spanish from the shadows. Why not go back to Mexico? he asked himself. He liked the country and the people. Why stay here and make a hopeless play against Beartrack?

He would have to fight his way past Havenrite and God knew how many more to reach the man he wanted. Was it worth it?

Then Kirk thought of Danny Dunster, buried in Chihuahua. He fingered the scar in the thick yellow hair above his right ear. The other scar at his back was the one that had nearly finished him. Yes, it was worth it. He'd face this man who called himself Sam Berryman.

When he thought of the man he felt an emptiness, for once he had liked Walt Chance. His thoughts went back to the first time they had met. Walt Chance, with his straight back and his confident eye, talking to Kirk and Danny Dunster about the horse ranch he had leased in Chihuahua.

"I've watched you boys break horses. I'd like you to work with me. I know the Barrios brothers, and they like our way of breaking saddle stock. Their own *vaqueros* ruin more than they break. We can buy cheap or trap the wild ones in the Sierras and then sell for a good profit."

In time the Barrios brothers, who owned a good portion of the state of Chihuahua, paid top money for the horses trained at Rancho Santa Margarita.

In those days Chance never talked about himself, only to say that he had been in the war and had fought mostly in Virginia.

Chance set a goal of two years. He said in that time they would have a stake and then he would go to Missouri. Although Chance never mentioned it directly, Kirk had the feeling that his older partner wanted to prove his worth to someone. A woman, perhaps.

Kirk was nearing the hotel when he caught a scent of lavender in the darkness of a slot between two buildings and heard a woman speak his name.

Chapter Six

KIRK TURNED to see Vanessa Berryman coming to the edge of the walk. In the glow of the kerosene lamp on the hotel porch above them he could see that she wore her black hair pinned up. Her green dress did not hide her shapely figure.

"I'd like to talk with you, Mr. Fallon," she said in the same rich voice he remembered.

He nodded. "I expected you to be on your way to Santa Fe."

"Plans change," she said, and made a graceful gesture with a slim hand. "Will you buy me coffee?"

She led him along the walk, the crowd in front of Oberley's turning from the discussion of the wounding of Bob Coleman to watch them and speculate.

She took him to a small café called La Ventana. They sat at a table by an adobe wall covered with cracked plaster. She sat with her hands clenched at the table edge. Her large eyes studied his face intently.

"At our last meeting you mentioned a name, Walt Chance," she said. "I want to talk about him."

"I know who he is, Miss Berryman. Havenrite told me."

Her thin dark brows lifted. "Then you've talked to Rex."

"Our discussion was interrupted." For a moment they were quiet. Talk buzzed about them. A fat Mexican cook leaned over the counter to talk to a *vaquero*. Kirk said, "You wish to talk about Walt Chance, Miss Berryman?"

She looked at him with an odd expression. "You talk like an educated man."

"I once planned to go to college—when I'd saved enough money breaking horses in Mexico with a man named Walt Chance."

"What did this man Chance do to you," she asked, leaning forward, "that you hate him so?"

He watched her for a moment; her face was pale in

the lamplight. Some Americans in range clothing took stools at the counter and loudly ordered a meal.

A waitress set coffee in front of Vanessa and Kirk. When the waitress had gone, Kirk told Vanessa about the horse ranch. "Chance was too greedy. He wanted all the profit for himself. One day I was in the corral breaking a horse. Chance shot me in the head and then in the back. Later I learned he had killed Danny Dunster at the same time. Chance took the money we'd saved, and the horse herd. By the time I was able to sit a saddle again, his trail was stone-cold."

"Now that you've found him, what do you intend to do?" she asked tensely.

"I intend settling with him."

"And to a man like you that means killing him!" she cried so loudly that those in the café turned to stare in surprise. The girl flushed at the stares her outcry had drawn. She unfastened a slender gold chain from about her throat, drawing from her bosom a locket studded with small diamonds. "This is worth at least three thousand dollars," she said hoarsely. "It belonged to my grandmother. Will you take it and get out?"

She dropped it in his hand, still warm from her body. He felt a quickening of his pulse and a moment of weakness. Then he thought of the gun trap in the Cobres, and his narrow escape from the violent end suffered by Ard Dunster.

He pushed the locket back to her. "I'm going to face Walt Chance," he said grimly. "He has a bill to settle with me. It's up to him how he wants to do it."

"I see." She sank back in her chair, biting her lower lips with strong white teeth. "As I said before you seem to be an educated man. At least you're different from the rest of the gunmen I've seen out here. And yet—"

"You're thinking of the ugly business with the Shatto brothers. Those two bodies weren't a pretty sight ror a girl, I'll admit. But I had no choice but to kill them."

"Can't I reason with you?" she asked. Her lips were very red. Her lashes were long, thick, and dark. "Can't I appeal to some finer side of you?" She tried again to get him to take the locket.

"It's no use," Kirk said firmly.

She put a hand to her eyes, then lowered it and peered at him. "I came to town hoping I'd see you." She straightened her shoulders. "To prevent more shooting, if possible."

"I'm sorry," Kirk said.

"Can't you understand that you're wrong about my father?" she said, trying once more. "He could never shoot a man in the back."

"But he did."

"You don't know him if you think that."

"I ranched with him for a year. I knew him. Do *you* know him?"

This seemed to stop her. "I didn't see him often until my mother died."

Kirk got to his feet, left a coin to pay for the coffee. "We could ride out to Beartrack together and face your father. Then you'd know the truth."

"You'd kill him," she said hoarsely. "As you did the Shatto brothers." She rose stiffly. "Will you take me back to the Lee House? We have town headquarters there."

Instead of leaving by the front door, she led the way to a rear exit that opened on a narrow alley, lighted dimly from lamplight off the main street. Her eyes hated him.

"I've asked you decently, Mr. Fallon, to ride out and leave my father alone. But you've refused, so—"

He felt a premonition of danger, but did not realize what she intended to do. Suddenly she ripped out the sleeve of her green dress, taking part of the bodice with it. He caught a glimpse of very white flesh. She began to scream.

Almost instantly the side door of the café was flung open and Vanessa cried, "Help me, somebody, help me!" She backed up, pointing an accusing finger at Kirk Fallon. "That man, he—"

The rest was lost in a roar as the men who had been eating in the café poured into the alley. The nearest started a hand for a gun. Kirk struck him in the face and watched the man collapse over a fire barrel. When Kirk pulled his revolver the rest of them drew up. There were shouts now from the main street, and the sounds of men running toward the alley, attracted by the scream.

"I didn't touch this girl!" Kirk shouted, but already a crowd was pouring into the alley, setting up such a clamor that it drowned out his voice.

Vanessa fled. Kirk, seeing a man lift a rifle, fired over the heads of the crowd, then turned and ran. The rifle sent a slug kicking adobe chunks into the back of his neck. He skirted a dark building, dodged along another alley past a blacksmith shop.

They came pounding after him, some of them shooting.

There were shouts of "Get the son! Head him off!"

Cursing Vanessa Berryman under his breath, Kirk sprinted for a row of sheds. Behind him men were shouting to one another in the darkness. They had lost him temporarily in the black maw of the alley. He tried to cut through a slot between two buildings so as to reach the horse tied beside the saloon. But some men were coming from that direction. He ducked into a darkened building entrance, held his breath as they roared past, some of them with lanterns.

There was an ominous sound to the tramp of their feet against the hard-packed earth, their excited angry voices. Their threats of what they would do to him.

He cut between two buildings, holding his gun straight down at his side, hat low over his eyes. He crossed the main street, unnoticed in the confusion. He angled across the dark plaza. They spilled out into the main street behind him, searching the shadows with their lanterns.

Up ahead a flaring kerosene lantern illuminated a black sign on the wall of an adobe building: "Cantina de los Amigos." He moved quickly that way, hunching over to make himself shorter, so that in the dark they might take him for a Mexican.

Kirk slipped into the cantina, empty save for a Mexican girl behind the bar. She smiled and said, "Do you wish to drink or to see me?"

"Is there a way out the back?" he asked.

She nodded, cocking her head at the noisy mob tramping across the plaza. He gave her a dollar and picked up a half-filled bottle of tequila from the bar. He took a long drink of the fiery liquor he had learned to stomach during his stay in Mexico. It sent the blood flaming through his veins.

A man jerked open the cantina door and shouted to somebody behind him, "Here he is!"

Kirk ran through a curtained doorway, past a workbench and cot. He heard shouting outside as he unbarred a door. He found himself in an alley, nearly tripping over a beer keg in the dark. A man coming abruptly around the corner of the cantina got the tequila bottle across the jaw before an alarm could be raised. They were coming through the cantina; he could hear the Mexican girl screaming at them to get out.

Kirk began running. A gun flamed. He put a feed store between himself and his pursuers and thus reached the alley beside the saloon. Ripping free the reins of his horse, he vaulted into the saddle. As he sent the horse rocketing into the thick shadows, a gun roared. He had not gone a mile before he heard pursuit in the moonless night.

With the hot wind in his face, he got the horse lined out for the mountains. Behind him a rifle crashed and he heard the awesome sound of the bullet not too far to his right. There was another shot and the horse faltered, but quickly regained its stride.

He reached the foothills through one of a dozen canyons and lost them in the darkness. He was in the first rugged country of the Cobre Mountains when the horse suddenly dropped, throwing him. It had been mortally hit back there, but had kept gamely on. Dazed from the fall, he listened for sounds of pursuit. Only the wind stirring the aspens. He stripped off his saddle and hid it, together with his rifle, in the brush, and marked the spot with a broken tree limb.

Gauging his position by the stars overhead, he began to climb through the mountains. At last he came to the wagon road, and he followed this until he wore a blister on his heel. He pulled off his boots and socks and walked barefoot in the thick dust. When he holed up in the junipers and tried to sleep, he found Vanessa Berryman's face constantly in his mind's eye. He damned her and was walking again at sunup.

He tightened his belt a notch; his stomach was grumbling. He'd had no supper last night, no breakfast this morning.

The sun rose over the eastern ramparts of the Cobres; aspen and juniper etched their greenery against the clear sky. It was midmorning when he heard angry voices up ahead.

Kirk felt a prickle of apprehension along his spine until he recognized one of the voices as Libby Squires'. The girl was laying the whip to somebody. He crept closer and saw the three of them sitting their horses at the edge of the road, Libby, Jed Purley, and Ramón Yáñez.

"I told you what would happen if you went after that

money," Libby told the big Purley. "I want nothing more to do with you."

"You'll get over it, Libby," Purley said hopefully. "Let's go up to your place an' I'll cook us up a meal."

"No. You wouldn't listen to me. I warned you to wait until we get some law in this country."

"You'll have gray in your hair before we get any law but the kind Beartrack wants," Purley said bitterly.

The horses caught Kirk's scent then and one of them nickered. The two men drove in the spurs, separating, coming up with their guns. Libby, looking startled, managed a wan smile.

"Hold it! Hello, Fallon."

Kirk moved up and saw the thick-necked Purley scowling at him blackly. Yáñez nodded a greeting. Kirk told them his horse had broken a leg and that he'd been forced to shoot it. He didn't say anything about the trouble in El Cobre.

"Wonder if I can ride double with one of you till I can get a horse," Kirk said.

Libby nodded. "I was on my way to Larnet's. You can ride with me."

Jed Purley holstered his gun and shook his head. "He ain't sharing no saddle with you," he said ominously.

Libby Squires narrowed her green eyes. "Jed, I told you it's all over."

"He can ride with me," Purley said, "or he can walk. Makes no difference to me."

Libby shrugged.

Purley's horse was not used to carrying double, and Kirk had a hard time hanging on behind the man. "I understand Havenrite's looking for you and Yáñez," Kirk said, and told them about Bob Coleman coming to El Cobre and how Havenrite and two of his men had ridden out vowing vengeance on the men who had shot the *segundo*.

Purley said, "Havenrite won't come up here unless he's got his whole crew with him. He knows we can blow him out of the mountains!"

"Your shooting Coleman," Kirk said, "is the excuse Havenrite needs to push your bunch clear to Mexico." He saw Purley's big shoulders tighten in front of him. "You should have listened to Libby," he finished.

Purley said over his shoulder, "I still ain't satisfied with your story about Pete and Charlie Shatto. So keep your mouth shut about our business."

Yáñez rode close, grinning. "Do not mind him," he told Kirk. "He is the jealous lover."

Libby said something under her breath.

There was a hoarse cry from Purley and he pointed suddenly ahead and said, "Beartrack!"

Five riders holding rifles had swung out of the timber to block the road. Another bunch came in behind Yáñez, who was bringing up the rear.

Rex Havenrite's voice boomed out. "Step down or we'll shoot you down!"

"Easy," Kirk called back at the big man in the striped wool shirt. "There's a woman here!"

Havenrite ignored him and rode up, the sandy-haired Bob Coleman at his side. The *segundo* was pale, shaken from the wound in his shoulder. His left arm was in a sling.

Libby's face had lost color. "All right, Rex, you've got us. Let's talk this over."

Havenrite ignored her again and repeated his warning. Either they dismounted or they would be shot. There was nothing else to do as long as they were under the muzzles of nine rifles, Coleman was the only one not holding a weapon on them.

Libby looked up into Havenrite's wide face, gauging the reckless anger in his eyes. "Don't do anything foolish, Rex," she warned, but her voice shook a little.

Havenrite put his hands on his hips. "You're quite an *hombre,* Fallon. I heard about Vanessa tearing her dress last night and claiming you got rough with her."

"I never touched her," Kirk said grimly, and wondered what chance they had against this group.

"Know what Vanessa did?" Havenrite said. "She come to Oberley's about midnight, when everybody figured to give up looking for you till sunup. She said she'd lied about you and that they were supposed to quit looking for you."

Kirk felt one of the men behind him ease his revolver from its holster. "I didn't think she'd be that fair," he admitted.

"That takes care of one problem," Havenrite said. "But how about you knockin' me into that table yesterday?"

Kirk tensed his muscles, knowing what was coming. "What about it?" he demanded.

Havenrite had picked up a coil of rope, and he suddenly lashed out to strike Kirk alongside the head with it. A blast of white light shook Kirk to his heels. But he recovered quickly and started for Havenrite. Some of the Beartrack men got him by the arms and dragged him to the ground. One of them kicked him in the head.

When he fully regained his senses he found he was sitting between Libby and Yáñez. Purley was beyond Libby. They all sat on the ground, hands roped behind their backs. Each one wore the loop of a saddle rope around the neck. Kirk could feel the rough hemp against his throat. He glanced at Libby. Her face was white.

They had all been taken some distance from the road. Beyond a clearing there was a large cottonwood tree with a stout limb. Kirk felt his throat tighten, but he would not give the staring Beartrack men the satisfaction of seeing his fear. He glared at them. His head ached from the kick.

"You're the bunch that shot Bob Coleman," Havenrite said, not looking at them.

"Rex, wait a minute." Bob Coleman stepped forward, but Havenrite turned on him.

"You were robbed and shot up, Bob. I want the bunch responsible to pay for it."

Coleman swallowed and looked startled. "But, Rex, you can't—"

Havenrite ignored him and turned to the stocky black-bearded Hank Ogden. "How shall we do it, Hank? All together or one at a time?"

Ogden spat on the ground. "One at a time. Make the bastards wonder which one is goin' to be next."

"Good idea," Havenrite said, and rubbed his hands.

Yáñez flung up his dark head to stare up at Havenrite. "I am the one who shoot Bob Coleman. Turn the others loose."

"Yáñez is anxious as hell," Havenrite said, jerking a thumb at Hank Ogden. "Get shut of him."

Ogden started forward with two other Beartrack men. They pulled the bound Mexican to his feet.

"My God, Rex!" Libby cried. "You've drunk with Yáñez. Camped with him. You can't do this."

Kirk was trying to free his hands, but the ropes did not give. The effort dampened his clothes with perspiration. "At least turn the Squires girl loose!" he cried.

Havenrite's brows lifted in mock surprise. "Girl? I don't see any girl." He turned to his men. "I see a long-haired boy, that's what I see." He turned to Bob Coleman, who looked sick, either from his smashed shoulder or from what he was about to witness. "What do you see, Bob?"

"A long-haired boy," Coleman said in a dead voice. The *segundo* turned his back and walked into the trees.

Havenrite frowned. "You ought to watch this, Bob. You're the one that got shot." There was no answer from Coleman. Havenrite jerked his head at Si Oldcamp. "Go keep an eye on him."

The lank Oldcamp nodded and went tramping off into the aspen grove, rifle swinging from a thin hand.

Kirk tried again. "The Berryman girl will hear about this. She won't like it!"

For a moment Havenrite seemed impressed by the possibility. Then he shrugged. "Things like this can be explained," he said easily, and gave Ogden a nod.

Yáñez was boosted, kicking, onto the back of his horse. Two men held the snorting horse, two others kept Yáñez in the saddle. The rope end was thrown over the cottonwood limb, tied to a sapling.

Knowing from the look on Havenrite's face that the man intended going through with it, Kirk said, "Don't watch, Libby." She was white and scared, sitting on the ground next to him. He didn't blame her. He could feel the frantic hammering of his own pulse. To live five years for vengeance and then die at the end of the rope on a lonely mountain slope . . .

He closed his eyes, tensing every muscle against the Mexican's scornful cry: *"Pelados! Hijos de putas!"*

The curse was abruptly checked; a horse ran quickly and was caught up. There was the creak of a tree limb, the twang of a rope suddenly weighted.

Libby Squires cried hoarsely, "Rex, if there's any justice you'll die the same way!"

Havenrite turned on her. "The Juniper Pool went too far this time. Stealing Beartrack money, shooting the *segundo*—"

Libby's mouth twisted. "Whose cows do you think you've been selling at Fort Bedloe? Your own?"

Havenrite jerked her to her feet. "You'll be next," he said in an ugly voice.

Purley let out a cry of rage and, despite his bound

wrists, got to his feet and tried to rush Havenrite. But the Beartrack men caught up with him and held him. Sweat poured from Purley's broad face. "You hurt Libby and I'll come back from hell for you, Rex!" he said.

Havenrite looked at him.

"Don't do it, Havenrite," Kirk warned; cold sweat drenched his back. "Hang a woman and you'll never ride away from it."

Havenrite, still holding Libby by an arm, said, "There's no woman here. I already told you."

Purley was white about the mouth. "He won't hang her. He'll make her squirm and think she's going to die. He'll make her sorry she didn't like his idea of settin' her up in a house in town once he marries that Berryman gal."

"Shut up, Jed," Libby said, never taking her eyes from Havenrite. Her body was trembling, despite the bold way she eyed Havenrite. "Rex knows that whatever was between us was over before the Berryman girl ever came here."

With an oath Havenrite shoved her to the ground. Unable to break the fall because of her bound hands, she fell heavily.

He turned on Purley. "Let's see how much yelling you can do, Jed," and Purley was dragged to the cottonwood and the end of the rope about his neck was tossed over the limb a foot from the swaying body of Yáñez.

Kirk heard a sound behind him and turned, seeing that Coleman, watching his chance, had sneaked out of the brush. Havenrite and the others had their backs to the two remaining prisoners, watching Purley being boosted into the saddle of his horse.

Coleman cut through Kirk's bonds with a knife blade. Then he freed Libby. He laid a gun on the ground beside Kirk. "Oldcamp's gun," Coleman whispered. "He won't be needing it. I'll stampede the horses. Good luck."

Coleman disappeared back into the brush. Purley was kicking at the men trying to hold the horse, shouting. Havenrite said, "Wait a minute. I want them on their feet to watch this."

He came back, long arms swinging at his sides. There was tension on his face, and behind him his men waited. Purley was in the saddle. One of the men held the rope end, waiting for Havenrite to come back before they tied it. A spooked horse could hang Purley before they were ready. They didn't want that. They were a hard-eyed lot, Kirk saw. And he wondered if all the Beartrack bunch was of this breed. Or whether this was a special crew, hand-picked for such work.

He let Havenrite get close. He wanted the man to haul him to his feet. Then he'd put the gun on him. Libby sat tense, pale, her hands held behind her back.

Suddenly from the trees came Si Oldcamp's cry: "Watch out for Coleman! He busted my head!"

Havenrite spun as there was a great clatter from the saddlers tied off in the trees. The horses bolted, crashing through the underbrush. As the men stood flatfooted, Kirk leaped to his feet, rammed the revolver against Havenrite's spine. Havenrite stiffened, looked back over his shoulder.

"Call your boys off!" Kirk shouted. "Or you'll have a hole in you big enough to step in."

Chapter Seven

KIRK MOVED so that he stood a little to one side of Havenrite, the cocked gun lined at a spot just above the man's wide shell belt. The Beartrack men had recovered from their surprise. They began to spread out a little. Oldcamp came staggering from the brush, streaming blood from a cut on the forehead.

Hank Ogden said from somewhere back in the trees, "Hang on, Rex. I can line my sights on Fallon."

Havenrite, peering back at Kirk, must have seen some change in Kirk's gray eyes. He cried, "Hold it, Hank. Damn it, my guts will get shot, not yours!"

The sounds of the stampeded horses came from a great distance.

Kirk said, "Tell your boys to shuck their guns. I won't ask you again!"

"All right, boys," Havenrite said, his voice tight with rage. "It's their play."

One of the men, sheltered by the aspens, suddenly opened fire. Kirk shifted the muzzle of the cocked gun as the bullet came whipping overhead. He fired in the direction of the gunshot and a man cried out suddenly.

Kirk put the gun back on Havenrite, who stood as if frozen. "The next slug will be in you."

Kirk was drenched with sweat, and his head ached from the roughing up they'd given him. Purley's horse, held by two of the men, suddenly went plunging off when the men released it to unbuckle their gun belts. Purley was trying to keep his saddle, gripping the barrel of the lunging horse with his knees. He swayed, his bound hands holding onto the lip of the saddle behind him. The long rope about his neck trailed like a snake, but did not catch in the brush. If it did later on, it would jerk Purley from the saddle and likely break his neck.

Bob Coleman came riding from the brush, leading Libby's horse. His narrow face was pale and tense from the strain he was under. "I tried to get another horse," he said to Kirk, "but I lost it. This arm doesn't help a man wrangle horses."

"Get in the saddle, Libby," Kirk ordered.

"We'll take Rex with us!" Libby cried.

It was Bob Coleman who shook his head. "Let's get out of here. This is Havenrite's old Cross Box land. Beartrack now, or have you forgotten? There may be more Beartrack men around."

Libby got into the saddle. The Beartrack men had thrown down their guns to glare at them. Kirk debated whether to send Libby to gather up the weapons. But one of the men might seize her for a shield. She'd been through enough for one day.

Havenrite looked at the sandy-haired *segundo*. "I'm going to get you for this, Bob."

Kirk stepped back, hit Havenrite a solid blow on the back of the head with his gun barrel. As he backed toward Libby's horse, he warned, "I'll kill the man who moves."

Nobody said anything. Bob Coleman held the reins in his right hand, together with a cocked gun. But if there was trouble the *segundo* would be at a disadvantage because of his bad left shoulder.

"Keep 'em covered, Coleman," Kirk said, "while I hit the saddle."

He finally reached the saddle, then took the reins from Libby. He pointed his revolver at Havenrite, unconscious on the ground from the blow on the head. "I'll kill him where he lies if any of you come after us."

"Come on, come on," Bob Coleman urged.

They backed their horses and then gave them the spurs. There was a shout from the Beartrack men. Kirk had a time controlling Libby's dun; it fought the bit, not liking the double weight. Libby screamed at it.

They reached the safety of the trees before the first Beartrack man picked up the gun he had shucked and fired. Bullets began slamming into the trees behind them. Kirk felt the breath of one beside his cheek.

Coleman was pounding along beside them. "It'll take some doing for them to get their horses!" the man shouted. "We'll have a headstart, anyhow!"

When they reached the road, there was no sign of pursuit. Coleman pulled up.

"You're on your own now," the *segundo* said seriously.

Libby leaned the back of her head against Kirk's chest. "Coleman, you're on our side of the fence now."

Coleman shook his head. "I got no use for two-bit outfits."

"You can't go back to Beartrack."

"Don't figure to," the sandy-haired man said with a trace of regret. "I always wanted to see California. Reckon this is as good a time as any."

Kirk had his hands locked around Libby's slender waist to keep her in the saddle in front of him. "We owe you something, Coleman. Thanks."

"I did it because of the woman—no other reason." He looked at Libby. His right arm had started to bleed again.

"You better come up to my place and let me bandage that arm," she urged. "Havenrite won't follow us up there."

Coleman shook his head. "Let me give you some advice, Miss Squires. You can't beat Beartrack. Give it up."

When he rode off, Kirk said they should try to find Jed Purley. They kept off the road, trying to see the man from the ridges. But all they saw was the Beartrack men, who had finally recovered the horses Coleman had stampeded. They were riding toward El Cobre. There was no sign of Purley.

"Hope he got away," Kirk said.

Libby didn't say anything.

At the edge of a high mesa she told him to pull up. When he did, she dropped to the ground. He followed her down, aware that her eyes were wet.

"A woman cries when she's happy or glad to be alive," Libby said brokenly, and turned over on her back and looked up at him, shading her eyes against the sun with a tanned forearm.

Nothing moved along their backtrail, only a trace of dust against the trees to mark their passage. He felt the tension go out of his limbs and marveled at his incredible luck in being able to survive in this rough country. He had faced a man with a shotgun and another man at his back. Last night he had shaken a mob off his heels. And today there had been a rope about his neck.

Libby suddenly flung her arms about his neck and pulled him close. "I try to be brave, but I was scared. When I think of dying, I—"

"Havenrite wouldn't have done it," he said, and stroked the soft flesh at the back of her neck.

"We'll never know whether he would or not," she said, and pressed her mouth against his throat. "When you die," she whispered, "you can never have the good things again. You can never love again." She lay back and looked up at him.

For only a moment did he think of Vanessa Berryman. Then he silently cursed the black-haired girl for what she had done to him last night.

"When you come close to death," he said, "you have an urge to make the most of every minute the rest of your life."

"Make the most of this one," she said, and he did. . . .

Later, at her small LS outfit, she cooked him a meal. She had run the place with her brother until he died, a year ago. Because of the hard lot of the mountain ranches, she had been forced to let the two hired hands go.

When they had finished eating, she suggested he spend the night, but he shook his head. She seemed disappointed. She regarded him for a long moment. "I didn't please you today?"

"You did. But I'm a drifter. I've been on the move too long to get tangled up permanently with a pretty woman."

"You've got to light someday." She began to unbraid her hair. "You could get the Shatto place cheap."

He borrowed a roan horse, the only good mount in her corral. She watched him ride out bareback, lifting a hand to him from the doorway.

In the hills below the Cobres he found his dead horse and the saddle he had cached in the brush. He saddled the roan, booted his rifle, and rode within four miles of El Cobre. There he bedded down on the hard ground, and got some rest. So great had the strain of the past days been upon him that he did not awaken until dawn.

He rode toward town with the sun at his back. He wondered if what Havenrite had told him was true. Had Vanessa confessed that she had lied about his tearing her dress? And even if she had, would some of the townspeople ignore it and still be after him?

He decided to take his chances. When he rode into the vast dim coolness of the Atlas Stable, his mind was set to rest by the fat hostler.

"We was sure hunting you last night, Fallon," the hostler said, taking Kirk's horse. "But then she said it was all a mistake." The man spat tobacco juice into a pile of straw at the edge of the runway. "Sure a hell of a thing for a woman to do to a man, wasn't it?"

"Yeah. How often does Sam Berryman come to town?"

"Why, he's here now." The fat man regarded him curiously. "You sure got everybody wonderin' about you, Fallon. You and Berryman have some trouble years back?"

"You might call it trouble," Kirk said, and hurried to the Lee House. The clerk had not expected to see him again, but the rent on his room had been paid up for a week. He went to his room and washed up and shaved and put on a clean shirt.

Then, smoking a cheroot, he went to the desk. "I understand Beartrack has town headquarters upstairs. Is Berryman up there?"

"No, he's over at Oberley's, likely telling the boys what's wrong with the cattle business."

Kirk looked at the narrow, pimply face. "You don't think much of Berryman?"

The man looked around the lobby, deserted now, then leaned across the desk. "How can you like a man who'll make a pauper out of his daughter, just so he can own a fancy ranch?"

Kirk said, "So it's his daughter's money."

"Her grandmother left it to her, is the way I hear it."

Kirk left his key and went outside and stood looking across the street at Oberley's Saloon.

Chapter Eight

SAM BERRYMAN, wearing a Denver-tailored gray suit, looked worried that morning as he stood at the bar in Oberley's. Some of those in the saloon attributed his drawn look to the shaky financial condition of Beartrack. There were those who claimed that even Rex Havenrite's consolidating his Cross Box with the larger ranch wouldn't save it. Cross Box had water, but to raise enough beef to make a ranch the size of Beartrack pay off you needed more graze.

Oberley tipped a wink to some men at a poker table. "You got everything running good out at Beartrack, Sam?" the saloonman drawled.

"I've been catching up on some bookwork," Berryman said, trying to make himself sound important and thus drown the note of worry in his voice.

The other customers tried to hide their grins. This business of "bookwork" was a standard joke. In the two years Sam Berryman had owned Beartrack he had shown a complete lack of ranching ability. Even the Englishman who started Beartrack had more savvy, it was agreed. The Englishman might have tried to ranch with insufficient graze and water, but he was smart enough to unload his white elephant. The valley had long ago decided that what Berryman knew about the cow business could be packed into an empty .45 shell case, with enough room left for a good-sized charge of powder.

Bert Wingate, who spent most of his time in town, away from his 6 Bar, glowered at Berryman from beneath thick white brows. "I hear your bunch hanged one of them pool men yesterday. Fella named Yáñez."

"I back up Rex in what he does," Berryman said, and with a trembling hand lifted a glass of whisky to his lips.

Wingate said, "I got a big investment over west of the the buttes, and I don't like the idea of a full-blown range war. Which is what we'll have if you don't call Havenrite off."

"I've given him full rein," Berryman said, and poured himself another quick drink.

"I got a feeling that Havenrite is deliberately stirring up that pool bunch," Wingate persisted, leaving the poker game where he had been sitting. He came up to Berryman on his short legs. "If things come to a head, you might get killed off. Then Havenrite would own Beartrack, lock, stock, and barrel." Wingate lit a cigar, peering up at Berryman's pale face. "Providing your daughter is fool enough to marry him, that is."

Berryman's shoulders stiffened. "Keep my daughter's name out of the conversation," he said with a trace of dignity.

Oberley winked and said, "Don't pull a gun on him, Sam. I got more holes in the roof now than I can patch before Christmas."

Some of the men laughed. Berryman flushed, knowing they considered him a fool and a coward and enjoyed riding him.

He said, "Anybody seen this Kirk Fallon who's supposed to be looking for me?"

"Sure, Sam," one of the men said. "He's standing right behind you."

And they all waited tensely to see what would happen.

Berryman turned slowly, color draining from his face. Men watched; cigar smoke drifted toward the low ceiling. Oberley, behind his bar, looked on with his mouth hanging open. Out in the street a man shouted at a dog.

Kirk Fallon said, "It's been a long time, Walt."

Sam Berryman's breathing was ragged. In his face at that moment there was little to remind anyone of the beautiful daughter he had sired. His face seemed to collapse.

Berryman looked around the quiet room. "It's no wonder I'm surprised, is it?" His voice was a croak. "I thought Kirk Fallon was dead. It's like seeing a man come back from the grave."

Nobody said anything.

"We've got some business to settle," Kirk said coldly. "Let's settle it. Then I'll be on my way."

Berryman followed him out to the alley beside the saloon, his feet dragging. He seemed old and shrunken.

"What is your name, anyhow? Walt Chance or Sam Berryman?"

"Berryman. I had a partner freighting goods over the old Santa Fe Trail to Chihuahua City. Walt died of the cholera down there, so I just used his name in Mexico. It was easier to take over his half of our business that way. He had no kin." Berryman mopped his face with a white linen handkerchief—paid for with his daughter's money, no doubt, Kirk thought.

"And I figured," Berryman went on, "that if I ever got in any trouble trying to make an honest dollar, then my daughter wouldn't be disgraced. It would be Walt Chance that did the deed, not Sam Berryman." He looked up into Kirk Fallon's hard face. "I lost everything in the war, Kirk. Those were mighty rough years. A man had to take what he could to get a stake."

"Quite a story," Kirk said, aware that men were peering at them from the side windows of the saloon.

"It's good to know you're alive, Kirk," Berryman said. "But from what Vanessa said, you don't think kindly of me."

"Of course I think kindly of you, Walt, or Sam, or whatever your name is. I think kindly of your poor aim. Had it been better, I'd now be buried down in Chihuahua with Danny Dunster."

"I didn't kill Danny. I didn't shoot you." Berryman licked at his lips with the tip of his tongue.

Kirk made an angry gesture. "You got rid of this Walt Chance as a partner, then you looked around for new ones. Danny and me. You knew we could break horses for you and do the dirty work. And when you got a herd and a little money, you got rid of us."

"Chance died of cholera!" Berryman cried.

Kirk said, "Be thankful I've met your daughter. If it weren't for her, I'd be tempted to take a gun to you."

"You don't remember what happened that day?" Berryman asked, his eyes a little wild.

"You shot me when my back was turned. You killed Danny!"

"No, Kirk, no! It was the Comanches. They sneaked up before I saw them. Luckily I was in the house and I fought them off. There were five in the party. I killed three and the other two high-tailed it, probably to get reinforcements."

"Now, why would they run?" Kirk's voice held a note of mockery. "Comanches aren't cowards. They were two to your one. They wouldn't ride off and leave a horse herd and fresh scalps, Danny's and mine."

"Something scared them off." Berryman's knees were shaking. "I dug up the money and took the herd. I figured to ditch the horses if they came for me again." He tried to smile. "You come out to Beartrack tomorrow and pick out enough horses to make up for your share."

Kirk removed the itemized statement from his pocket. Berryman stared at the figures, his mouth falling open as he read aloud: " 'Total owed Kirk Fallon by Walt Chance, seventy-eight hundred dollars.' "

"That's beyond all reason!" Berryman cried.

Kirk's mouth hardened. In the street a man had pulled up a wagon and was standing up, watching them. Other men were looking on from the walks, trying to overhear, speculating on what would happen. Kirk ignored them.

"I spent five years hunting you," Kirk said in a low, tense voice. "I could have had a wife maybe and an outfit of my own. You owe me something for those years."

"I only committed one crime, if you can call it that!" Berryman wailed. "I ran off and left you. But I knew Danny was dead. And I thought you were gone. Your head was all bloodied. And I was so afraid those Comanches would come back that I was half crazy. I've got an unholy fear of Indians. I get a smell of one and my nerves go all to pieces."

With the flat of a big hand Kirk pushed the smaller man against the saloon wall, held him there. "If your conscience is so clear," Kirk said thinly, "why did you pay the Shatto brothers to try to gun me?"

"It wasn't me, it was Rex." Berryman clamped his lips shut.

Kirk said, "Another score I'll settle with Havenrite before I clear out of here." He removed his hand from Berryman's shoulder. "You better thank God that Dunster got his up there in the mountains. Because he planned to kill you. And maybe I couldn't have stopped him. Even if I'd wanted to."

Berryman had both hands pressed to his face.

Kirk said, "I want that money. All of it. You've got till midnight tomorrow."

"We haven't got it."

"Borrow on your cattle."

Berryman's lips were pale. "I've got the biggest sprea in these parts behind me. I can have thirty men ridin you down." Berryman seemed close to tears. "I'll mak a reasonable settlement. But seventy-eight hundred do lars!"

"I should collect more for Danny Dunster. But Dann had no kin, only Ard. And now Ard is dead. So we'll le it go for what you owe me."

"Kirk, you can't threaten me this way!"

"If you send Havenrite after me, I'm going to kill hin Tell him that!"

Kirk turned on his heel and pushed his way throug the gaping men on the walk. He moved rapidly across th plaza, heading for a cantina. His nerves were jumping and he felt sick at his stomach. He needed to get drunk. Some how the moment he had dreamed of—facing Walt Chanc again—was flat. And he knew why. Vanessa.

Chapter Nine

The following day Kirk Fallon restlessly prowled the streets of El Cobre, glancing occasionally along the road that led to Beartrack. The sky above the mountains was a vivid blue. Heat was reflected from the thick adobe walls of the business structures. The citizens of El Cobre regarded the tall, grim, yellow-haired man as some sort of evil omen. His coming here intensified the strife that gripped the country.

Only Bert Wingate of the 6 Bar spoke to him. It was midafternoon and Kirk was watching two drunken teamsters Indian-wrestle in front of the Giant Store.

Wingate drew Kirk aside and said he'd been asking questions about him. "Ran into a drummer who said he was in Borden, Kansas, when you cleaned it up, Fallon. Tough town."

"It was a tough town," Kirk agreed, thinking of the badge he had turned in upon receipt of the letter from Pete Shatto.

"Maybe that drummer isn't the only one around here who knows your rep with a gun." The small rancher tipped back on the built-up heels of his boots and regarded Kirk coolly. "Maybe that's why you haven't got a Beartrack tombstone on your chest by this time."

"So?" Kirk watched one burly teamster throw his adversary into the street. Then, the wrestling over, the two men weaved across the street and batted their way through the swing doors of the saloon.

"You've got Havenrite to fight," Wingate said. "I don't know what your business is with Berryman, but—"

"You're right. My business is with Berryman, not Havenrite." Kirk felt irritated at the probing. "But if Havenrite gets in my way—" He didn't finish it.

"I've watched Rex grow up," Wingate said. "He's a rough boy. He set up there in the mountains on his Cross Box and laughed at that poor Englishman who started

Beartrack. Then when Berryman took over, Havenrite moved in."

"I hear you were doing some laughing yourself, Wingate," Kirk said. "You wanted the Englishman to go broke so you could pick up his ranch for next to nothing. You're hoping the same for Berryman."

"I could operate both ranches and show a profit," Wingate admitted. "What I'm getting at is this. If you think you're going to take one two-bit piece out of Beartrack without tangling with Rex Havenrite, you've got another think coming."

Some sunbonneted women came out of the Giant Store and stood talking a moment on the walk, then went their separate ways. Thunderheads were building up over the Cobres.

"You're not telling me these things because you like me," Kirk said. "What's on your mind?"

Wingate tried to hide his anger. He was used to having people listen to him. He told Kirk that there had been no law since the town marshal died last year. "I think you could get the job, in view of all your past experience."

"No job," Kirk said bluntly. "I intend to collect what Berryman owes me and move on."

"With a badge you'd stand a better chance of collecting," Wingate persisted.

"What's your interest in this?"

"I've got no love for Beartrack or the Juniper Pool. If that mountain bunch want to run cows on a shoestring, it's their business. But if there's real trouble, we'll all be involved." Wingate spat over the edge of the boardwalk. "A lot of my six Bar boys have been with me for years. They're not gun-slingers. I don't want to bury any of them."

"So you want me to take a badge," Kirk said thinly, "and fight your battle for you."

"With a badge," Wingate reminded him, holding down his temper, "Beartrack would think twice about killing you."

"Thanks, but I'll handle it my way."

Havenrite came riding in from the west, the silverwork on his shell belt catching the sun. A big man on a sorrel horse, he cruelly reined the animal in at the walk in front of Kirk Fallon and Wingate. Several men on the walk stepped hastily into doorways; others peered out of windows.

Havenrite swung down, braced his thick legs. "Fallon, you've got till sundown to get out of El Cobre."

"I guess I hit you over the head harder than I figured," Kirk said easily. "Because you ought to know by this time I won't be scared out."

Havenrite tipped forward his hat, rubbed the back of his head where Kirk had struck him down. "I haven't forgotten that," Havenrite said. "I haven't forgotten a lot of things. You remember what I said."

Turning abruptly, he led the sorrel across the street and tied it at the rack in front of Oberley's. Kirk watched the man's broad back as Havenrite shoved his way into the saloon.

Wingate, standing at Kirk's elbow, said, "A lot of folks around here are getting tired of Rex. He's got a tough crew at Beartrack. Not like the bunch that was there when Berryman bought the place. I had a quiet talk with some of the boys last night at Oberley's. Your name was brought up. The badge is yours if you'll take it."

"If I took a badge I'd be obligated to stay around. Even after my business with Berryman is settled." He was thinking of Vanessa Berryman, and how her eyes had hated him the other night. "I figure to head on west when it's over. There's nothing here to hold me."

"You better let me buy you a drink," Wingate snapped, "because it's probably the last chance I'll have."

"I'll take that drink later," Kirk said.

"You won't be around to drink it," Wingate said. "You're a stubborn man, Fallon. And it's the stubborn ones who fill boothill."

Kirk went to the plaza and listened to a fat Mexican play a *guitarón*. As he listened to the music, he realized that the back of his shirt was wet, and that there was so much tension in his right arm it ached. He had been so sure that when Havenrite swung down from that sorrel it meant a showdown.

He thought of the other times he had faced men like Havenrite. There had been no perspiration soaking his shirt then, no tension in his arm. No fear. What had changed? And he knew what it was. Somewhere in life a man met a woman, and suddenly staying alive was much more important to him than it ever had been before.

He walked south out of town, past the Mexican quarter, where half-naked children shouted and chased mongrel dogs and chickens ran squawking in and out of adobes.

His long search was ended, and it had turned sour in him. Chance or Berryman or whatever his name was had turned out to be a pathetic figure of a man, laughed at because he had allowed an Englishman to unload a white elephant of a ranch on him, and had purchased it with his daughter's inheritance. In desperation, as the money dwindled, Berryman had taken in Rex Havenrite as partner in order to have access to mountain water. And now Berryman had a puma by the tail; Havenrite's ambition threatened to blow up the country.

He smoked a cigar in anger and tried to recall that last day at the horse ranch in Chihuahua. He tried to do this in fairness to Berryman. When he had regained consciousness after the shooting, he found himself in the house of a Mexican family many miles from the ranch. They had found him, they said, when they came to sell hay. They had found Danny Dunster dead in the barn and buried him. They had not mentioned finding any dead Comanches about the place. Kirk had never questioned them, for he had been positive that it was his partner that had killed Danny and left him for dead.

Then he swore softly. Of course it was Berryman. No one else could have shot him. This talk of Comanches was to cover up. Now Berryman was. frightened of this past that had suddenly confronted him, and might make him a thief and a killer in the eyes of his daughter.

And Berryman had called on his partner and future son-in-law to frighten Kirk Fallon out of the country.

As he turned back toward the center of town he recalled Havenrite's order to be out of town by sundown. That wasn't like the man at all. It was more like Havenrite to have pulled a gun there in the street and tried to settle the thing. For Havenrite, he was sure, was no coward. And from what Kirk had overheard around town, the man had a natural ability with a gun.

Kirk steeled himself with a new resolve: to see this thing through. Berryman had until midnight to settle. Not that Kirk thought he would. But he had given the man that deadline. After that, new plans would have to be formulated.

He was eating his supper of *taquitos* and *carne seca,* which he generously soaked in *salsa picante,* when a Mexican boy gave him a message. Vanessa Berryman wanted to see him at the Beartrack town headquarters in the Lee House.

Flipping the boy a half dollar, he paid for his meal in the cantina at the south end of the plaza and went out into the darkness.

Over the Cobres the moon hung thin and yellow. Lamplight glowed in house windows. He heard someone chording on a guitar. A woman laughed.

There was a knot of tension at the back of his neck as he climbed the stairs to the Beartrack suite, overlooking the main street. On the second floor he shifted his gun in its holster. He was sweating. Fear again? It might be the girl. It might be Havenrite waiting for him with a cocked gun in his hand.

Vanessa's voice told him to enter in answer to his knock. The room was large and tastefully furnished, with a long horsehide sofa against one wall, a sideboard with bottle and glass on the other. Above the sideboard was a portrait of a younger Sam Berryman in a gray captain's uniform of the C.S.A.

Behind a flat-topped desk sat Vanessa Berryman. She wore a pale-blue dress and about her throat was a necklace of pearls. A lamp, with a flowered design on the glass shade, burned at one end of the desk.

He closed the door and stepped quickly to an inner door and peered down a short hallway to two separate bedrooms.

"We're alone," she said in her rich voice, and inclined her dark head toward the sofa.

He sat down and crossed his long legs. "Do you plan to rip the sleeve out of your dress and start screaming?"

Strong white teeth sank into her lower lip. "I'm sorry about that," she admitted. "All I wanted to do was discourage you from facing my father—perhaps killing him."

"I nearly became permanently discouraged," he said. He fiddled with the brim of his hat, balanced on his knee.

"When I realized the awful thing I'd done, I told the men the truth." She folded her hands. Her fingers were long and the pink nails glistened in the lamplight. "They didn't think much of me, you can be sure. It was an awful thing to do. I realize it now."

"I gave your father a deadline. Midnight tonight."

"He discussed it with me." She flushed. "He was frightened, and—well, he had been drinking. Otherwise I probably wouldn't know the details. He's never talked things over with me. But in his condition . . ." She let her voice fade.

"Havenrite also gave a deadline. Sundown. He said I was to be out of town."

She studied him across the desk, a flicker of a smile touching her lips. Then it was gone. "You don't frighten easily."

"I'm glad you realize that."

Kirk waited, listening for any suspicious sound on the stairs, in the hallway. In the street below a drunk howled; there was the sound of someone emptying a bucket of water into the alley beside the hotel.

"Rex and I had a nasty scene," Vanessa said. "I have his promise not to—to kill you."

"You have the money with you?"

"I am going to ask you to go away, Mr. Fallon."

"No."

She lifted a slim hand. "Let me finish, please." She looked regal sitting straight in the chair, bosom softly stirring against the blue fabric of her dress. "I will give you an I.O.U. for the amount you think my father owes. When we have the money it will be sent to you."

He gave her a cold smile. "You have cattle. I'll take enough to satisfy the debt."

"That won't do," she said. "The herd is our only asset and—"

He got to his feet. "Because of your father I've wasted five years of my life."

"Mr. Fallon, have you ever read the Bible?"

"Some."

"Then you know the value of forgiveness."

"I also remember the part about 'an eye for an eye.' "

She rose, her eyes narrowed, watchful. "You expect me to feel sorry for you because you dedicated five years of your life to vengeance? Hasn't anyone ever told you such a life will turn you old and bitter before your time?"

Suddenly he hated her. "You revile me, but what about the man you plan to marry?"

She swallowed, looked down at the desk. "If Rex can save my father—"

"Berryman is lower than I thought if he'd expect his daughter to marry a man like Havenrite. A man who put a rope around the neck of a woman and threatened to hang her."

"It was only bluff." Her voice faltered. "Rex told me all about it."

"Libby Squires wasn't so sure but what he'd have gone through with it."

"You can't believe a woman of her reputation, one who goes from one man to another."

"I'll take her word any day against Havenrite's."

She came around the end of the desk, her skirts rustling. She faced him, hands clenched in anger. "I'm going to tell you something, Mr. Fallon. I'm not at all sure my father owes you any money at all."

That was as far as she got, for he caught the scent of lavender from her hair. He put his hands suddenly on her silk-clad arms. She looked up at him, startled. Then he drew her against him and found her mouth. He could feel her teeth under her stiffened lips. She tried to struggle. Then the lips relaxed. And then he was surprised at the animal strength in the long body as she arched, trembling, against him.

He released her and heard himself say, "That was payment for the torn-dress business."

A bright anger flashed into her eyes and she struck him across the face with her open hand. They stood facing each other for a moment, then tears came to her eyes.

In that moment he was suddenly aware of a breeze blowing against the back of his neck. He whirled. Rex Havenrite stood in the doorway, his amber eyes thin and ugly. Behind him in the hallway were other men.

"A trap," Kirk said, "a dirty trap," and he went for his gun.

Vanessa screamed as they rushed him. Kirk's gun, half out of its holster, was torn from his grasp. They drove him against the wall. Seizing one man by the throat, Kirk hurled him backward, scattering the others. Fighting them off as they moved in again, Kirk ripped a revolver from the holster of the nearest man. Another Beartrack man snatched a bottle from the sideboard and hurled it. Kirk ducked but the bottle struck his right arm, numbing it. He dropped the gun.

The black-bearded Hank Ogden came in from the left,

another man from the right. Kirk slugged Ogden in the face. The man dropped to one knee. The other man caught Kirk on the back of the neck. They all bore him to the sofa, but he struggled out from under their weight, using fists and his knees. There were shouts from downstairs, the sound of boots pounding on the stairs.

Kirk gained his feet. Something crashed against his jaw. He went to his knees. He saw their faces, hard, grimly determined to finish him. He pawed about for his fallen gun. A man caught him around the neck from behind. A fist exploded against his ear. He lunged forward, sank his teeth into the muscled calf of a leg. A man cried out.

They jerked him to his feet and his head cleared long enough to hear Havenrite yelling, "I told him to clear out of town by sundown!"

Kirk tried to use his head as a battering ram. He knocked the breath from one man. Another lay unconscious under the desk. Hank Ogden had recovered from the smashing blow to his face. Blood trickled through his black beard from a cut lip. As Kirk fought, he got behind him and with his own thick arms pinned Kirk's to his sides.

"I got him!" Ogden was shouting.

They came at him, pounding at his ribs, his kidneys. He sank down and a boot crashed against his cheekbone.

He didn't remember when they got him by the ankles and dragged him down the stairs and out into the alley.

He awoke with lantern light in his eyes and whisky in his throat. There was a crowd peering down at him. He gagged on the whisky, but life flowed feebly through his aching body once again.

Ed Oberley, wearing his saloonman's apron, passed him the bottle again. "Fallon, you've had your warning."

"The hell with 'em," Kirk said thickly. "Next Beartrack man I see I'll shoot."

"Don't be a fool," Oberley said seriously. "The girl kept them from killing you."

"I kissed her and all the time she knew Havenrite was out in the hall!" Kirk tried to get up. He fell back.

"No smart card player mixes in a game he can't win," Oberley said. "Get out of town."

"Show me my horse," Kirk Fallon mumbled.

When it was brought up they pushed him into the saddle. He rode out into the night, heading toward the Cobre Mountains.

"Wonder if he's got sense enough to keep on going," a man said.

"Not him," Oberley said. "I've seen his kind before. Before this is over, him and Rex will stand toe to toe and shoot each other to pieces."

"And if that happens, Bert Wingate will get Beartrack, like he's always wanted. All he's got to do is just sit around and let it fall into his hat."

Oberley took a drink from the whisky bottle he had brought for Kirk. "I feel sorry for the girl. Havin' a father like Sam Berryman must make her have nightmares."

"You mark my words. She'll marry Havenrite and Beartrack will own everything up to the Rim. In six months there won't be no Juniper Pool. And in six days there won't be no Kirk Fallon. Rex ain't goin' to face up to him. Not when he can hire it done. Even a gun hand like Fallon, good as he might be, can't fight thirty men."

"Amen," Oberley said. "Let's go over to my place and drink to Fallon. He handled them Beartrack boys rough tonight. Doc Graham's workin' on a broken arm, a split skull, and a busted ankle."

Chapter Ten

VANESSA SLEPT very little that night. At daybreak she rose and put a wrapper over her nightgown and went to the window that overlooked the mountains. The ragged bulk of the forested slopes was frightening. The people up there were a threat to her very existence.

She turned and rested on the window sill and looked at the room with its thick carpeting, ornately carved bedstead, marble-topped commode. She fingered the thick velvet window drapes. The Englishman who had built Beartrack and furnished it had had good taste.

And her father had wanted it all for her; to make up in two years what he had failed to give her earlier in life. She remembered her mother saying once, "When Grandmother leaves you her money, don't ever let your father have it. Not a penny. Understand?"

But he had come to her in St. Louis and told her of this wonderful ranch. Well, he was her father and there was no one else left in her family.

As she dressed she thought of Kirk Fallon. He was a man who lived by his gun. When she had first seen him, with two dead men, he wore rough clothing and needed a shave and looked like a thorough ruffian. But last night . . . She pressed a hand to her lips, trying to remember his kiss.

Then, angrily, she dropped her hand. How could she pretend even for a moment that she had enjoyed the brief incident last night? This man had come here to blackmail her father. And if that failed, to kill him.

She went down the hallway to her father's office, surprised to hear voices at this early hour.

She paused outside the door, hearing Havenrite say, "All right, then *you* take the herd to the fort next time, if you think I'm handling it wrong."

"It isn't that, Rex, but—"

"You know something, Sam? You're scared to go.

You're scared one of those 'Pache bucks over there will get within five feet of you."

"It isn't so," Berryman said too loudly.

Havenrite laughed. "I remember last year when those bucks jumped the reservation. You lost ten pounds worrying that six Indians with poor horses and three rifles between them would hit Beartrack." Havenrite added thinly, "You got Injun fever, Sam. Why for?"

"It goes back a long time," Berryman said. Then, "But we're talking about Beartrack, not Indians." He cleared his throat. "I understand you've threatened to shoot Bob Coleman if you find him."

"Sure, Sam. He was working with the Juniper Pool. Has been right along."

"I can't believe that, Rex. I hear it's because he wrecked your hanging party the other night." There was a moment of silence, then Berryman added, "One thing I'm beginning to learn about you, Rex. You lie mighty easy at times."

"The same for you, Sam. Lying that you didn't shoot Kirk Fallon in the back."

"I didn't, I tell you. It was Comanches."

"And if it was," Havenrite went on easily, "it was a hell of a thing to do. Ride off and leave a partner without even burying him."

Vanessa opened the door and both men looked up.

Her father was red in the face. "We were talking about your going to Santa Fe for that visit."

"I know what you were talking about," she said, and wished she had not spoken so sharply, for her father got a sick look in his eyes. She turned her attention to Havenrite, wondering now if she could ever bring herself to marry him.

"Rex, this violence has got to stop," she said.

"This is violent country," Havenrite reminded her. "We've got the pool waiting to jump us. Wingate hates us and is sitting on the fence waiting for us to go under. And somebody rides out of your old man's past and tries to get seventy-eight hundred dollars out of us." He lifted his heavy hands. "Either we stand up to these folks or they whip us."

"That was a despicable thing you did last night, Rex. Six men on one."

Havenrite shrugged. "I saw Fallon go to your room. I

figured to teach him a lesson. I told him to be out of town by sundown. I could have used a gun on him."

"Why didn't you fight him man to man, if you objected to his kissing me?" she demanded.

Havenrite had been peering absently out the window to watch some Beartrack riders drive a herd of horses into one of the corrals. Now he wheeled slowly, the skin tightening over his prominent cheekbones.

"Kissing you?" he said softly. "That must be something I missed. Tell me about it."

Fear stabbed her as she realized Havenrite had not seen her in Fallon's arms. "It was an accident," she murmured, trying to pass it off. Havenrite continued to stare at her. She felt the blood rise to her cheeks. "I want this trouble with the pool stopped," she said defiantly, to hide her embarrassment.

"Now, honey," her father said soothingly. "You let Rex and me handle this."

She stared at this slightly built man who was her father. Had her mother been right all those years? "Your father could have made his fortune here in St. Louis," her mother would say. "But he is prey to anyone strong. A man comes along and says there's gold in Peru or silver in Nevada. And your father forgets his family and leaves and we send him money and—"

"Do *you* approve of the way Rex is handling things?" she asked her father quietly.

Berryman picked up a bottle from the desk. Vanessa shuddered as she watched him take a long drink.

"We've got no choice but to go along with Rex," he said.

"If you'd gone to Santa Fe like you planned," Havenrite said, "all this trouble would be over by the time you got back."

"By hanging men? By shooting them?" Her eyes were furious.

Berryman said, "If it hadn't been for Rex coming in when he did, every dollar I have in the world—"

"Every dollar *I* have in the world," Vanessa corrected him, and hated herself for saying it. He looked so pitiful. "I have a plan."

They listened to her outline her project. She wanted to give a dance and barbecue here at Beartrack on the following Saturday. Everyone was to be invited, the members of the Juniper Pool, the townspeople, the other ranchers in the West Basin. Everybody.

"I want them to know that we're not ogres here," she went on.

"And I suppose you'll sweet-talk the pool into moving off their land so we can use their water and their graze for our herd."

"We don't need that land, Rex," she said firmly.

"I'm negotiating for a beef contract that will make us the biggest shippers in this part of the country."

Sunlight streaming through the window brought out the lights in her blue-black hair, the defiance in her eyes. "We'll trim our herds. We'll raise only enough beef on Beartrack for the amount of graze and water we own."

Havenrite looked at her as if she had lost her mind. "You'd rather Beartrack be a two-bit outfit? You'd rather lose all the money you've dumped into this ranch?" He sounded incredulous.

"I'd rather lose every dollar"—she started to say every dollar that her father had spent foolishly—"that *we've* spent foolishly. We can get along with half the men we have now. We can live simply. No more trips to Denver and living high on the hog."

Berryman stared at his daughter as if seeing her for the first time. "But, honey, you've always been rich. I didn't think you'd ever know how to live simply." He lifted his slender hands in a helpless gesture. "I didn't think you'd know how."

"Grandmother wasn't always rich," she said.

Havenrite lost his temper. "Do you think you can dance with that pool outfit and feed them barbecue? Why, they'd laugh at us."

"Who started it, Rex?" she asked calmly. "Who really started it?"

"What do you mean?" Havenrite's mouth was hard.

"Did we steal their cattle first? Or did they steal our money?"

Havenrite colored. "You can't drive cattle over the Rim without picking up strays. I've offered to pay them for the cattle we've accidentally picked up. But they yell 'cow thief.' And it gave them an excuse to turn outlaw and steal our money. Not that they needed much of an excuse."

"You were one of them once," she reminded him.

Something leaped into his amber eyes that frightened her, and she wished with all her heart that her father, in a moment of weakness, had not given this man an interest in Beartrack. She said firmly, "I want my way in this." Then she turned to her father. "I also want this matter settled between you and Kirk Fallon."

"With a gun at my head?"

"Work out a sensible arrangement, then let him be on his way."

Havenrite, watching her closely, said, "Fallon's left the country. He was seen going up over the Rim this morning."

Vanessa paled, straightened her shoulders. "Then that matter, at least, is settled. Will you see that everyone is invited to the dance, Rex?"

Havenrite gave Berryman a guarded look. "I'll see that it's taken care of. But don't be surprised if none of the pool shows up."

"On second thought," Vanessa said, looking into Havenrite's bland gaze, "I'll tend to it myself."

"It's a fool thing you're planning," Havenrite warned. "It won't take more'n a long-drawn breath to send everybody shooting at each other."

"It's up to you to see that doesn't happen," she said, and went out.

Havenrite caught up with her in the hall. "We could be married Saturday. Then there'd be a real excuse for a shindig."

"No, Rex, not Saturday."

"Still thinking of Fallon?" His voice was ugly.

He suddenly pulled her into the circle of his arms. His strength drove the breath from her. When he released her and said, "Better than Fallon's kiss, huh?"

She glared at him.

"You better say it, Vanessa," he told her. "If you don't, I'll hunt him down and kill him if it takes ten years."

She forced a smile to hide her sudden fear. "I'm going to marry you, not Fallon. That should be answer enough." Then her eyes narrowed. "You gave me your promise never to take a gun to Fallon. If you do, I'll never marry you."

She swept past him and ran to her room. She thought, If I don't marry him he'll wreck Beartrack. And it will kill my father.

She stepped to the window and peered out at the mountains rising in their jagged splendor to the sky. She wondered which way Fallon was riding, and if, in the years to come, he would remember her at all.

Chapter Eleven

FOR TWO DAYS Kirk Fallon lay in the big double bed in a corner of Libby Squires' one-room house, seven miles up in the Cobres from Larnet's Store. She had found him passed out in front of the store and brought him home. At first she thought he was dead, he was that beaten. But his strength returned rapidly.

On the morning of the third day she moved about the room, wearing a gingham house dress and moccasins on her small feet. She fiddled at the stove, her braids jiggling against her back. She had not spoken to him all morning.

"You're angry," he said. He was propped up with two pillows behind his head.

She turned on him, her cheeks coloring. "I'm not very flattered," she snapped. "Last night you called me Vanessa."

He shrugged. "You hate a person and sometimes the name slips out at the wrong time."

"It was the wrong time, all right." Her green eyes were angry. "And don't tell me you hate her. I know better."

"She got me off my guard so Havenrite and his boys could jump me. If she hadn't, there'd have been some dead ones in that room."

Libby seemed to soften toward him and gave him a good noonday meal and laced his coffee with some bourbon. She sat on the edge of the bed while he ate and studied his bruises. Considering what he had been through, he seemed in remarkably good shape. Better than some of the Beartrack men, she had heard down at Larnet's Store.

Within the hour he had two visitors. The first was a drab, graying woman who looked as if life had lashed her to a post.

Libby said, "Kirk, this is Irma Shatto."

It wasn't an easy moment, facing the wife and sister-in-law of men he had killed.

"I hold nothin' against you, Mr. Fallon," the woman said dispiritedly, "I knowed Pete was fixin' to earn hisself some easy money. And he'd shoot a man in the back for it. Charlie wasn't no better. At least Pete can't beat me up of a Saturday night when he comes home from Larnet's Store full of mountain whisky."

The woman sighed, and turned to Libby. "Just stopped by to tell you I'm goin' to Tucson to live at my sister's. Ain't no use tryin' to run the ranch alone. Maybe I can peddle it for something one of these days."

Libby talked with the Shatto woman and made coffee for them all. Kirk felt of his money belt. It was a wonder he hadn't been robbed when he lay unconscious in front of Larnet's Store after the long ride up from El Cobre. Which he didn't remember at all.

"How much will you take for the place, Mrs. Shatto?"

The woman looked surprised, and reminded Kirk that he had already given Libby five hundred dollars to pass along to her. "That'll keep me for a spell. You ain't obliged to buy the place."

"How much?"

Libby said, "In all fairness, Pete let the place run down. How many head of cattle there are I couldn't say. But—" Her eyes were shining. "I think you could make something out of it, Kirk."

The Shatto woman licked her lips. "Would—would fifteen hundred dollars be too much?"

He paid over his money and accepted a quit-claim deed, together with the widow's thanks.

When the woman had gone, Libby smiled and said, "You're my neighbor now."

"I'm not sentimental," he said gruffly. "That's not why I bought the place. But I know Berryman isn't going to settle without a fight. The Shatto ranch will give me a base of operations, an excuse for hanging around this country. I'm not going to let him rest easy."

Libby smiled and kissed him. "You like to make people think you're tough."

He clutched the quit-claim deed in his hand, feeling the thrill of ownership that had so long been denied him. And he remembered what Vanessa had said about five years out of his life dedicated to vengeance. He had put down his roots at last.

The second visitor was Vanessa Berryman, who wore a

wool shirt, and boy's black trousers that had been altered to fit her long curved body. She came with five Beartrack riders, who remained in the yard.

When she saw Kirk Fallon sitting on the porch with the Squires girl, her brows lifted. "I heard you'd left the country, Mr. Fallon," she said coolly.

"Hardly," he said.

She twisted her hands. "I—I'm sorry about what happened that night. It seems as if I'm always bringing you trouble. Rex had no right to—"

"Just hearing you say it," Kirk said, making his voice hard, "has healed my aches and pains."

His tone seemed to hurt her. It was Libby that asked coldly. "Just why did you come here?"

Vanessa told them about the dance and barbecue Saturday.

"You want to show off Beartrack's strength," Libby flung at her, "so we'll realize we have no chance."

"I have a plan and I'll announce it at the party. Please come."

"Maybe you think I'm afraid to," Libby said, "because of Rex. Well, let me tell you, I was through with him before you came here. You didn't take him away from me."

Kirk, seeing the confusion on Vanessa's face, said, "Tell us why you think this dance is a good idea."

She did her best to convince them to come without revealing her project.

"It'll be a good day for your father to settle up with me," Kirk told her.

"I'm still not sure of what really happened in Chihuahua."

"Danny Dunster was killed. He was a good boy. He wasn't like his brother Ard. But no matter who shot Danny or me, the fact is that your father ran. He left me dying, and if some Mexicans hadn't found me—"

"My father has an inordinate fear of Indians," Vanessa said. "It goes back to his youth. Something that happened to his older brother, my Uncle Ruben, whom I never saw. So it's possible he was panic-stricken when the Comanches hit your ranch."

"If they *did* hit it," Kirk said. "We'll see you Saturday, Miss Berryman."

Kirk felt oddly touched when she rode out with her men, her dark head held high, shoulders straight. And he thought, She's only a girl and she's carrying a load too big for most men.

Libby, watching his face, said, "Don't tell me you're not falling in love with her."

"In love with the daughter of a killer and a thief?" he said in anger. He walked through the aspen grove, working the stiffness out of his legs.

"Now, look at it this way, Jed," Rex Havenrite said. "I lost my head the other day. Sure I hanged Yáñez, but then, he's the one that shot Bob Coleman."

"You don't give a damn for Coleman," Jed Purley snapped. He was sitting his saddle at the edge of the road to El Cobre, ten miles south of Larnet's Store. He had his hands lifted under the threat of the cocked rifle held in Havenrite's big hands.

He had been drinking Larnet's whisky all morning. He was in a sullen mood. His eyes were bloodshot. The lock of coarse brown hair arched from under the brim of his dusty hat. He had been coming along the road, letting the horse pick its way, head down, thinking of Libby and the crazy happenings of the past few days. Havenrite had been on his sorrel, waiting at the edge of the road. Havenrite put the rifle on him before Purley could reach for his revolver.

Purley had spent the first three minutes cursing Havenrite. Surprisingly, Havenrite had taken it, showing his inner rage only by the thinning of his amber eyes.

"You don't give a damn about Bob Coleman," Purley said again. "I hear you got some boys up on the Rim lookin' for him."

Havenrite shrugged. His sorrel cropped grass. The aspens were golden in the noonday sun.

"We used to be friends," Havenrite said. "When I lived up here."

"You'd put your own sister in a crib if it'd make you a dollar."

"Shut up, Jed," Havenrite said without anger. He still held the rifle. "We've got a common enemy and I want to talk about him."

"Who?"

"Kirk Fallon."

"He'll be gone from here. The hell with him."

"That's where you're wrong. The Shatto woman came

through town this morning. She said Fallon bought her out yesterday."

Purley scowled and his slow brain tried to digest this startling fact. Fallon was a drifter. It was strange he'd tie himself down to a seedy outfit like the Shatto place. "What of it?" Purley demanded.

"He's living up at Libby's. Been there three days now."

Slowly the blood drained from Purley's face. "I warned him," he said, a thin rage working into his voice.

Havenrite spat. "I want him dead, or so crippled up he'll never be any good as a gun-fighter."

Jed, in his anger, was capable of only one thought at a time. "Livin' up there under Libby's roof! I'll kill the son!"

"Or beat him up. You're a tough man, Jed. Nobody's ever whipped you yet that I know of. I wouldn't want to fist-fight you, that's for sure."

Now Jed Purley was reached. "You scared of Fallon?"

A muscle twitched under Havenrite's left eye. "Let's say that if I go after him, I lose Vanessa. I want to marry that girl. If I kill Fallon, or if I get some of my boys to do it, she won't marry me."

"You could make her do it. You get everything else you want."

Havenrite shook his head; his chin strap swayed across his wide chest. "You can buy a woman or you can force her. But you can't make her love you." This was embarrassing talk, but he had to make the dim-witted Purley understand. "I don't want the Berryman girl to hate me."

"So you want me to kill your snake for you."

"That's about it."

"What do I get out of it?"

"A good price for your spread, yours and Libby's. I'm moving into the mountains. I'll buy out Old Man Hoskins and you two. Nobody else. You'll have money enough to take Libby away from here. To a place where she can forget Fallon. And everybody else she knew up here." Havenrite was referring to himself in the last part of it.

Purley said, "I'll ask around. If what you say is true about Libby and Fallon, you don't have to worry none."

Havenrite said, "There's going to be a dance at Beartrack Saturday. Fallon will be there with Libby. That might be a good time."

"Why there?"

"Then everybody could see that I had nothing to do with Fallon's getting shot up or beat up." He booted the rifle. He kept his eyes on Purley, though. He wasn't afraid of the man's gunwork. Only his fists he respected.

"You want the Berryman gal looking on when I finish Fallon, is that it?"

"You've got it, Jed," Havenrite said, smiling. "You're a smart one to figure that out."

"I'm dumb as hell and you know it," the man said sourly.

"Come on and ride into town. We'll drink a bottle together at Oberley's and talk about that new life you and Libby are going to have someplace else."

Purley hesitated, his narrow forehead ridged in a scowl. "I hate your guts, Rex."

"Don't blame you," Havenrite said, and neck-reined his horse into the road.

"But I'll drink your whisky. I ain't got a dollar in my jeans. And my credit's run out at Larnet's."

"Let's go, then," Havenrite said.

"You ride ahead. I don't trust you at my back."

Havenrite laughed, but took the lead on the road that led down out of the mountains to El Cobre.

Chapter Twelve

NEXT MORNING Kirk rode with Libby to take a look at the property he had purchased. In the distance the Rim seemed a solid wall of rock rising above the timber. They entered a canyon and crossed a mesa; he saw in the distance the deserted line shack and thought of Ard Dunster, buried there. When he thought how near he had come to death that day he felt a cold hand at his back.

The Shatto brand was the Spur, and it was the only fancy thing about the outfit. He thought of the day he had ridden up here with Dunster, and how Pete Shatto had come down the broken steps of the porch. He crossed the weed-grown yard with Libby and entered the house. The walls were stained with cooking grease. There was the stale smell of unwashed bodies. Kirk unbarred the rear door and opened the two windows to air the place out. Behind the house a cliff rose sharply; halfway up was a wide ledge, reached by a slanting path from the roofless barn.

There were no horses in the corral. Irma Shatto had taken the work team and sold her husband's mule and the other horses. Kirk asked Libby if she minded if he kept riding the roan he had borrowed from her for a few more days. She shrugged. She seemed preoccupied. Last night he had slept in the barn. It had made her angry.

They rode on up to the eastern boundary of his ranch. On the way he counted thirty-five head of scrawny cattle in his brand. He hadn't bought much, but it was something to build on. Maybe some of the government land farther up would be open to filing one of these days. Or maybe he could lease some sections . . . For the first time since Chihuahua he felt a measure of stability.

They were just about to turn around when Old Man Hoskins and his two lank rifle-carrying sons rode out of the junipers.

"You better sing out your brand after this," the gray-bearded old man advised. He was booting a rifle. "You're on my land."

"Sorry," Kirk said. "I'll watch it after this."

"Hear you bought the Shatto place," Hoskins said.

"Yep."

"You buy in when the smart ones are plannin' to get out of the country."

"You one of the smart ones?" Libby put in.

The old man flushed. His two sons sat their saddles, long legs hooked over the horns, rifles across their laps.

"You better watch out," Hoskins told Kirk. "Beartrack's after your scalp."

"They wouldn't be this far up," Libby said.

"There's about ten of 'em up on the Rim," Hoskins said, and waved a veined hand toward the wall of rock behind him. "I hear they're layin' for Bob Coleman."

Kirk's mouth tightened. "I thought Coleman was out of the country."

"Well, Coleman stopped at my place the night of the Yáñez hangin'," Hoskins said. "He'd lost a lot of blood from that shoulder and wanted to swap horses. Well, I told him that seein' as how I personally hadn't had no trouble with Beartrack, I wasn't fixin' to start none. So I sent him on his way."

Libby showed her disgust. "That was a pretty heartless thing to do."

The oldest Hoskins boy, a long-jawed towhead, leered at her. "Now, you wouldn't want us Hoskinses to get in no trouble with your sweetie Havenrite, now would you?"

Kirk said, "That's enough of that."

The boy unhooked his leg from around the horn, leaned forward in the saddle holding his rifle. "Did I hear right, mister?"

Old Man Hoskins said, without turning his head, "This here is Kirk Fallon. You better mind your manners."

Obviously the boy had heard of Fallon, but he was stubbornly angered. "I ain't used to people tellin' me to shut my mouth." He spoke with a high twang.

"You'll learn," Kirk said, "or you'll learn how to handle a gun better than you do now."

The boy started to shift the rifle. Kirk's revolver leaped into his hand. The boy's mouth fell open. Carefully he lowered the rifle. He didn't say any more.

Kirk holstered the gun, said to the old man, "If you

see Coleman, tell him to come down to my place. I'll put him up. He saved my neck the other night."

"I'll tell him. Likely he's holed up in one of them old Indian caves," Hoskins said. "Unless he's got past them Beartrack men. Which I doubt."

They were about to leave when Hoskins said, "Ain't none of my business, Fallon, but if I was you I'd watch out for Jed Purley. I—er—well, he knows where you been stayin' of a night."

The older Hoskins boy was grinning, looking Libby up and down. She appeared not to notice.

She said, "I'll have a talk with Jed and put him right about a few things."

"And I seen Jed Purley and Havenrite drinkin' together at Oberley's yesterday," the Hoskins boy said, grinning again. "Purley was so fulla whisky you could've wrung a gallon out of his sock."

Fallon said, "You need glasses. Havenrite tried to hang Purley. You don't drink with a man who tries to kill you."

When Hoskins and his sons had moved up through the trees, Kirk said, "I don't blame Purley for getting drunk after the way I moved in."

Libby's green eyes flashed. "You didn't move in. I wanted you. I told Jed we were through after he took a gun—" She broke off, looking worried. "It's just the sort of cute thing Rex would do. Play Jed's hate."

"Purley's not that big a fool."

"That's just the trouble. He is."

Kirk said, "Can you make it to your place alone?"

"I've been doing it for years. Why?"

He told her he was going up on the Rim and have a look for Coleman.

"But there are Beartrack men up there."

"If it weren't for Coleman, I wouldn't be here." He patted the stock of his booted rifle. "I'll keep my eyes open."

An hour later he was on a bald rock at the base of the Rim. Here he had a good view of the valley. Below, at a distance of a mile or so, was a ranch, probably the Hoskins place. To his right were a series of caves. He moved that way, and when he was under the first one he saw what he thought was blood. Dismounting, he looked for further sign and saw a rabbit skin and some bones. Somebody had blown the head off the animal with a .45 slug, and eaten the flesh raw. Somebody was hungry. The blood he saw on the rock belonged to the rabbit, not to Coleman.

He moved cautiously along the line of caves, halting under each one and calling softly, "Coleman, it's Kirk Fallon."

There was no answer. He was angling back toward the road when he ran into three of the men who had been in the hanging party the other night. The nearest was Si Oldcamp. The trio was startled by his sudden appearance, but instantly they dug in their spurs and went for their guns.

As they separated, Kirk fired the rifle and Oldcamp's horse plunged over the lip of a short cliff, throwing the man down a shale bank. The other two had reached a stand of pines, where they turned to fire on him. Kirk tried for a tall redheaded rider, but his bullet only ricocheted against a rock. The second man had flung himself from his horse. Kneeling, the man worked the lever of his rifle and began to fire. Kirk lay over the roan's neck and sent the animal over a clump of sotol. Oldcamp had retained his gun in the fall, and now he was leveling on Kirk from the bottom of the shale bank.

Realizing the odds were too great with all of them trying for him, Kirk cut off through some junipers. He did not pull up until he was nearly a mile down the road. He sat his saddle, straining his ears, but there was no sign of pursuit. Then he began cursing Vanessa Berryman. She had talked about peace on the one hand while her men tried to murder him on the other.

At first he decided against attending the dance. Then he wondered if she really knew what went on at Beartrack. If she didn't, it was time she learned.

For two days he stayed away from Libby's, working around his own place, trying to get the grease smell out of the house. On Friday one of the pool members came by to say there was to be a meeting at Larnet's Store that night.

When Kirk arrived at the store he found Jed Purley sitting on Larnet's bar, drinking whisky out of a tin cup.

Purley got to his feet and the bald Larnet said, "Easy now, Jed. Take it easy."

Two other pool men were drinking at the bar. They stepped hastily aside to take up positions of relative safety behind the big stove. Purley wore a revolver. His gaze was intense, his mouth a tight slit. He looked wider than usual in his loose-fitting range clothes.

Kirk tried to ignore Purley, but the man wouldn't have it. "I hear you're one of us now," Purley said, and set down his tin cup on the bar. He turned to Larnet. "Since when you lettin' into the pool a gent whose mother had pups?"

There was an immediate silence in the big store. Insects batted the big copper overhead reflectors.

Kirk said, "Mister, that's the same as calling me a son-of-a-bitch."

Purley swayed and Kirk realized he was quite drunk. His eyes were bloodshot, puffy. "Well, let's argue it, then," Purley said thickly. He balled a heavy fist and started for Kirk. Drunk as he was, the man was formidable. He was wide as a barrel and nearly six feet tall.

Kirk backed up and drew his gun. "I've had enough rough treatment in this country. I'm not taking more of the same from you." Just as quickly as he had drawn it, Kirk holstered the heavy revolver. "Step outside and repeat what you said in here. But if you do, have a gun in your hand."

Purley blinked his eyes. "The hell with you," he said, but he made no move to go outside.

Kirk hooked thumbs in his belt. "Purley, you talk a big wind for a man seen drinking Havenrite's whisky."

Purley seemed surprised that anyone knew about his drinking with Rex Havenrite.

One of the men behind the stove said, "What about that, Purley?"

Purley had a stupid look on his face. Confronted with facts he did not know how to defend himself with words.

"You better explain it, Jed," Larnet advised.

Purley jerked down his hat on his hound skull and tramped to the door. "Guess I know who my friends are!" he shouted, and ran down the steps. He spurred a horse cruelly off into the trees.

Larnet came up to stand beside Kirk. "Don't ever make the mistake of fist-fighting him, Fallon, He's the best saloon brawler in these parts. He may be empty in the head, but he's got bull strength."

"I'll remember," Kirk said, and stepped to the bar and had a drink.

"We got some new blood in the pool now," Larnet said later, when the pool members had assembled. "Kirk Fallon. I've told you before the only way we can keep Beartrack out of these mountains is to shoot every one of them we find north of the hills."

There was a murmur of assent. Libby, who had come in quietly, stood against the wall. She wore her Levis and shirt. Her hair was in braids. She did not speak to Kirk.

Larnet turned to Kirk. "When the trouble first started, I was on the fence. Beartrack used to come up here and trade. But when Havenrite became a partner, he ordered the men to stay away from here. Well, that took a chunk out of my profits. And then one thing led to another." He munched on a wedge of yellow cheese. "I've loaned money to some of the pool. So besides liking these boys up here, I've got a financial stake in this."

Kirk said, "Let's give the Berryman girl a chance to tell her story at the dance tomorrow, before we go loading up our guns." He had decided to say nothing about the three Beartrack men he had run into up on the Rim.

All eyes were on Kirk, but it was Larnet that said, "You've got your own fight with Beartrack. They try to hang you and beat you up. And now you want to talk peace."

Libby Squires spoke for the first time. "I don't like the Berryman girl, but Kirk talks sense. We can't lose anything by seeing what she's got up her sleeve."

Most of them had been against attending the dance, but Libby won them over.

Kirk went over to her, smiled. "Are you saying that for yourself, or because you think it's what I'd like you to say?"

The green eyes looked up into his gray ones. "I've missed you," she said quietly.

"It's better that I stay at my own place," he told her. "There's already enough gossip."

"That's something I'm used to."

The men were discussing Beartrack and how the crooked major at Fort Bedloe let Havenrite sell cattle in any brand as long as he got his cut.

"Show me a bluecoat with braid on his shoulder, and I'll show you the biggest thief north of Austin," one of the pool men with a Texas drawl put in.

"All Army officers aren't thieves," Kirk said.

"Guess you haven't met many. Or else you fought on the bluecoat side."

"I did," Kirk said, thinking of the years when he had marched into the deep south and his idealistic views after Appomattox, which seemed silly now. When he had tried to be friends with the people he had helped to conquer. And had been rejected in most cases. Until he met the soft-spoken Southerner who called himself Walt Chance. After that had come the tragedy in Chihuahua.

He felt the old anger rise in him again. How could he have been so wrong about a man? Of course, he had been younger then, but . . .

He went out to the veranda and stood in the glare of the kerosene lamp over the door. He was staring into the darkness, rolling a cigarette, when he caught movement in the trees beyond the store. Instinct caused him to fling himself to the porch. A rifle crashed and a bullet knocked splinters from the doorframe.

Before he could free his gun, there was the sound of a horse crashing off into the trees, and a high-pitched Rebel yell.

Kirk was picking himself up when the pool members rushed outside with their rifles. Larnet blew out the lantern above the door so as to make them less visible targets.

"Maybe it was Beartrack," one of them said nervously.

"That sounded like Jed Purley," Larnet said with a shake of the head. He looked at Kirk. "If I was you, I wouldn't stand at a window of a night with a lamp at my back."

When the others had gone back inside, Libby hugged Kirk's arm. "I'm scared to stay alone," she whispered. "Either you come to my place or I'm coming to yours."

He looked down at her shadowed face. "Once you get your claws in a man, there's no getting away."

Chapter Thirteen

It was early afternoon before Kirk and Libby Squires arrived at Beartrack. He was surprised at the crowd milling about the yard. Japanese lanterns had been strung above tables and benches. There was a delicious aroma of roasted meat coming from the barbecue pits, where stones had been heated to cook the meat.

Vanessa, wearing a gray dress with red trim at collar and cuffs and hem, seemed prettier than usual. Kirk felt a wrench that they had so little in common. In the first place, he despised her father. But aside from that, she was rich and had been raised without privation, and that dress alone had probably equaled the price of three months' staples at the store for one of the mountain ranchers like himself.

She took Libby into the big stone house, where riding clothes could be exchange for a dress.

Oberley, the saloonman, came up attired in his Sunday suit. He said, "You didn't take my advice and clear out."

Kirk shrugged. "I'm in deeper than ever. I bought the Shatto place."

"So I heard. You sure must like trouble, Fallon."

Libby came out of the house, wearing a green dress that matched her eyes.

Ray Larnet, wearing a brown suit, said, "I'd forgotten how good-looking you are, Libby," and claimed her for a dance. At the far end of the yard three musicians, playing concertina, fiddle, and banjo, started the dancing with a waltz.

Kirk caught sight of Jed Purley on the wide porch that ran the length of the house. He saw the stricken look on the man's face as Libby and Ray Larnet danced together. And Kirk thought, He really loves her.

The pool members moved awkwardly in the crowd. Kirk saw Havenrite talking to Old Man Hoskins. It seemed odd that men who had threatened to shoot each other could now have an apparently rational discussion. Some of the other pool men were standing around listening to Havenrite. Perhaps Vanessa was wiser than anyone thought in giving this dance.

Somebody pressed a bottle into Kirk's hands and he took a drink, then had a plate of barbecued beef. He saw that Vanessa was busy seeing that the children had sweets, supervising the serving of the barbecue.

When the guests had eaten, Vanessa came up, looking very grave. "I hope you won't try to settle anything with my father today," she said in a low voice. "I want this to be an occasion for building friendships, not destroying them."

Before she could accept or reject him, he caught her up when the music started again. He whirled her out onto the hard-packed portion of the yard that had been set aside for dancing. She felt light in his arms, and there was a disturbing scent of lavender from her hair.

But he couldn't push aside his old anger when he caught a glimpse of Sam Berryman on the porch, talking to Jed Purley.

She must have sensed his thoughts, for she tilted back her head and looked up at him. "You hate my father don't you?"

"What he did is not an easy thing to forget." And then he was sorry he had let his feelings show in regard to Berryman. When he was away from her, all he could think of was being near her. But when they were together, it was the old feeling against Berryman that dominated his thinking.

"You bought the Shatto place," she said, "not to better yourself, but so you'd be in a position to turn the country against my father." Her mouth was an angry red line. "I suppose by this time you've told everyone what you claim he did to you down in Chihuahua."

"You kept Havenrite and his men from kicking me to pieces the other night," he told her. "For that I thank you. Let's leave it at that."

She said nothing, but when the music stopped she moved through the crowd and was claimed by an El Cobre merchant who danced with more whisky in his blood than grace in his feet.

Despite the outward gaiety, there was an undercurrent of tension. There was no outward display of firearms, but

Kirk noted that most of the pool members, like himself, wore coats despite the September heat, to hide their revolvers.

Kirk found Sam Berryman on the porch, sitting beside a small table that held a bottle. He did not look at Kirk.

"For years I dreamed of finding you," Kirk said, sitting on the porch rail. "I planned how I'd make you pay. But now I guess I'll have to give you some time."

Berryman shot him a look out of his bloodshot eyes. "That's the first decent thing you've said to me."

"Only because of your daughter."

Berryman reached for the bottle, then let his hand fall at his side. He stared out at the couples dancing, those at the long tables still eating. Children ran shrilly through the yard.

"Last night Vanessa asked me all about you," Berryman said thickly. "She wanted to know how you were in Mexico."

"What did you tell her?"

"I said you had ambition. That you wanted the money we made there to go East to college. You'd only been out of the war two years then, but you didn't have that cold look in your eye that makes men afraid of you. That came later."

"Because of you," Kirk said. "I liked you. I don't remember my own father. You were older. I looked up to you."

Berryman picked at a broken fingernail. "And you think I ruined all that, don't you?"

"I'd like to believe that it was Comanches," Kirk said. "But I'm sorry, I don't."

"How can I convince you?"

"No man could live on the frontier and be so frightened of Indians. A man like that should live in a city."

Berryman looked at him. "Havenrite knows how Vanessa feels about you. He doesn't like it."

"And how about you?"

"You and she could never mean anything to each other. There's too much between you. She's a proud girl. She'll marry Rex and save this ranch and save me."

"If you let her do that, you're more of a coward than I thought."

"She'd become a pauper. I couldn't support her. What would she do? She has no relatives but me."

"You're even less of a man when you're drunk," Kirk

said, and gave the bottle on the table a slap with the tips of his fingers. He saw Havenrite come out of the house and give him a cold look.

Kirk was about to go down the steps into the yard when he saw Jed Purley pushing his way through the crowd to the porch.

"Fallon, you rode in on a roan horse," Purley stated. He did not seem drunk today. "It looks like a horse I been missing for a spell. Let's go check the brand." Kirk felt a tautness in his chest as the crowd quieted. The music stopped. All eyes were on them.

Libby was elbowing her way to the porch rail. "Kirk, I'm sorry," she said, biting her lips. "When I loaned you that roan I didn't stop to think—"

Purley, never taking his eyes from Kirk, pushed her gently back into the crowd. "The brand, Fallon. Let's go look at the brand."

"Don't bother looking," Kirk said, and took a deep breath. "It's got an Angle Iron brand."

"I got a bill of sale for that horse!"

The silence thinned. Men crowded up, some of them gleefully at the prospect of a fight. No party was complete without at least one brawl. Mothers were herding their children to the far end of the yard.

Havenrite moved up behind Kirk on the porch. "I guess Purley doesn't like the idea that Fallon moved in on his woman."

Somebody laughed. There was a shifting of feet.

Vanessa ran lightly up the porch steps and caught Kirk by the arm. "Please don't ruin everything by fighting with him."

But Purley, standing in the yard, looking up at the porch, said, "Fallon, you're a damn horse thief. What you aim to do about it?"

While the crowd looked on, Kirk debated. He still had not fully recovered from the beating at the hands of Beartrack. His hands were stiff and his ribs were still so sore that it hurt him to take a deep breath. He saw Libby trying to talk to Purley, but he couldn't hear what was said. Purley ignored her. Beyond the tables the Mexicans were looking up from their barbecue pits. Heat waves rose from the rocks that had been used to roast the beef. Kirk gave Vanessa a tight smile and put both hands on the porch rail.

"Purley, I've got a hunch Havenrite put you up to this. Don't play his game. He was going to hang you the other night. Or have you forgotten?"

"He's crazy jealous!" Libby cried, and tried to grab Purley's wrist. He flung her off.

Purley said ominously, "Come down here, Fallon, or I'll come up and get you!"

And in that moment Kirk Fallon thought, What am I doing here? Why have I let myself get into a position where I'll have to fight for a woman I don't love? He thought of the empty years hunting his ex-partner, the refusal to put down his roots. And at last he had reached the end of the trail. Instead of a quick settlement either with gun or with money, he had bought into a range war. For he realized now that nothing Vanessa Berryman could do or say would stop the shooting. Havenrite was in too deep.

He turned his head and saw Sam Berryman watching him. A weakling. A man you couldn't shoot because he wouldn't have the guts to draw against you. He shifted his gaze to Vanessa, seeing the clean part in her dark hair, the paleness around her mouth.

"Please don't do this," she said in a low, tense voice.

"A man called me a thief," he reminded her. "This isn't my doing," he added, and started down the porch steps.

Somebody—probably Havenrite, he thought later—put out a foot. Because he was so intent on watching Purley's eyes for any overt move, he did not see the foot until too late. He tripped and plunged headfirst down the remaining steps. Purley kicked him so hard in the neck that he was flung over on his back.

"Fight!" a man squealed, and Purley drove in hard with the heels of his boots.

Vanessa was screaming, "Stop it, somebody!"

Kirk rolled aside as Purley tried again to stomp him. His head was clearing. He got to his knees, swayed away from Purley's clubbing fist. Purley kicked at his face. As the swinging boot toe swept past his cheek, Kirk grabbed the ankle. He stood up with it and Purley was spilled on the back of his head. He lost his hat, and his hair, powdered with dust, fell across his forehead.

One lesson Kirk had learned in his years of knocking about the frontier: If you have to fight, end it quickly. There were no ethics involved in beating a man before he beat you. He was mindful of Ray Larnet's earlier warning about Purley's prowess as a saloon brawler.

Still clinging to Purley's ankle, Kirk came in quickly. He intended to kick the squirming man in the head. But at that moment he caught sight of Vanessa and saw the look of revulsion on her face as she guessed his intention.

It froze him. His moment of indecision allowed Purley to kick himself free and regain his feet.

Dust rose, and horses, tied off beyond the barbecue pits, snorted and tugged at their ropes. Kirk blocked a right and took a left to the stomach. They grappled. As they swayed across the yard, the crowd broke behind them. Kirk felt Purley's muscles strain, felt perspiration from the man's narrow forehead spray his face as Purley tried to butt him on the nose. Kirk crashed down his own head. Their foreheads met and both men reeled. But Kirk recovered more quickly. He rushed after Purley, wanting to end it, for Purley was solidly muscled and long of wind and they could spend an hour senselessly smashing each other to pieces.

Libby screamed, "Kirk, the bottle!"

And at that moment something smashed him between the shoulder blades. As he dropped sickly to his knees, the whisky bottle that had struck him down skidded across the yard. Twisting his head, he tried to see who had thrown it, but the bank of excited faces revealed no clue.

Momentarily stunned, he was wide open for Purley's lifted knee. It caught him on the jaw. Dazed, he tried to seize a leg. Purley fought him off. Kirk struggled through a barrage of fists and got to his feet. Desperately he tried to hit the man, but his arms were leaden. For an instant he was struck with the awesome possibility that the blow to his back had partially paralyzed him.

Sensing victory, Purley closed in and belted him so hard on the jaw that he was driven over one of the tables. Kirk lit on his back and rolled aside as Purley came around the end of the table. A blast of intense heat struck Kirk's face. He found himself on hands and knees, peering down into one of the barbecue pits.

Purley had seized an olla from a table and tried to bring it down on Kirk's head. Kirk ducked. The olla crashed against the rocks in the pit. As the clay container broke apart, cold water was splashed over the heated rocks. A great cloud of steam rose from the pit.

Still dazed from the blow of the thrown bottle, Kirk tried to crawl away, but Purley got him around the neck. A great cry of protest roared out from the crowd as Purley, in his insane rage, started inching Kirk toward the pit. Seized with panic, Kirk clawed at the thick arm about his throat. Purley moved him another step toward the pit.

In a sudden move Kirk twisted free and flung his weight against Purley's knees, driving the man against a table, smashing it. Enraged by the attempt to drop him into the pit, Kirk got Purley by the hair before the latter could extricate himself from the fallen table. Kirk smashed him in the face. Purley groaned, spat out a tooth, and tried to cover up. Kirk was after him. Purley, dripping blood from a gashed cheek, reeled away. He tried to slug it out, but Kirk struck him so hard the man's knees buckled. Purley fell against him and his weight drove Kirk to the edge of the pit. Purley seemed out on his feet.

For an instant Kirk debated. He could twist aside and let Purley drop into the pit. And the crowd seemed to sense that he was weighing a decision. Their eyes were wide, mouths open. In that moment a breeze tore aside the curtain of yellow dust kicked up by the boots of the two men.

"Drop him, Fallon!" a man shouted. "That's what he tried to do to you!"

Suddenly Kirk flung Purley aside and the man fell loosely, away from the pit. Breathing heavily, his back aching from the blow from the bottle, Kirk waited for Purley to get up. The man's eyes were open and he looked at the smoking pit, where the steam was still rising. Then he looked at Kirk.

"All right," he mumbled through cut lips. "You beat me. And to hell with you." He fell back and lay still.

A man pushed a bottle into Kirk's hand. Kirk took a long pull. His coat was torn, his shirt in shreds.

Vanessa came up. Her face was pale. "I don't blame you for what happened, Kirk."

Libby fought her way through the crowd, her green eyes angry. "Tell your father better luck next time!" she cried at Vanessa.

Vanessa was startled. "What do you mean?" she demanded, and the guests crowded around in anticipation of a brawl between two females.

"Your father better improve his aim," Libby said thinly.

"If he'd hit Kirk on the back of the head with that bottle, Purley would have finished it."

"You saw my father throw it?" She was incredulous.

Libby hesitated. "No, but he had a whisky bottle in his hand just before it happened. I saw that much."

"My father wouldn't do such a thing," Vanessa said, with a lift of her chin.

Kirk had had enough. "No, he'd just shoot his two partners and leave one of them for dead. And steal money and a herd of horses. But he wouldn't throw a whisky bottle at a man's back!"

Vanessa looked hurt. "I find you a very hard man to like, Kirk Fallon!" she cried, and whirled, sobbing, into the crowd.

The pool members and their families lost their stomach for the party. They rode out with Kirk and Libby without giving Vanessa a chance to explain her plan for bringing peace to the range.

Somebody back in the crowd said, "Well, him and Purley fought like a couple of bulls over a cow. Reckon we know who she belongs to now."

Kirk turned in the saddle and tried to identify the speaker in the crowd watching them leave. Libby said, "Forget it, Kirk."

As they rode into the foothills, Libby seemed unusually gay. "That Berryman girl is pretty impossible, isn't she?" she said, and cast Kirk a hopeful glance. If she wanted him to agree, she was disappointed. He said nothing. She bit her lip and appeared to concentrate on the trail that curved up through the junipers.

When they reached her place, Kirk said tiredly, "You'll be safe enough here alone. Purley won't hurt you. He's in love with you."

From the porch of her house she watched him ride out. Then, with a hopeless shrug, she turned into the house.

That Berryman girl, she said to herself. He can't get her out of his mind. No matter what the Berryman tribe does to him, he still loves her.

She kicked at a chair and then flung herself down on the bed and wept.

Chapter Fourteen

KIRK RODE DOWN to Larnet's Store and bought a dun horse that had been left there for sale. He left Purley's roan for the man to pick up.

With a bottle of whisky in his saddlebag, Kirk rode for home. He felt tired in every muscle. And his face ached from the pounding of Purley's fists.

It was dark by the time he reached his own place. For five minutes he waited on a knoll and studied the yard, bathed now in moonlight. No shadows moved. The dun's ears did not twitch as he rode down the slope, a rifle in his hands.

After fixing himself a meal, he blew out the lamp and went to the veranda to smoke a cigar. He watched the distant cliffs bathed in moonlight, listened to the wind stir the strees. He heard his horse neigh as a bobcat screeched somewhere higher in the timber.

A sound caused Kirk suddenly to throw his cigar over the porch rail. It hit the ground and burst into a shower of sparks. He swore softly at his foolishness in giving away his position. He was on his feet, gun in hand, peering toward the aspens that were massed darkly under the moonswept sky.

He saw a blob of something white moving in the trees. Then he heard the sound again; boots trampling brush.

"Who's out there?" Kirk said, and stepped three paces to the right to confuse anyone who planned to use the sound of his voice as a target.

"It's Bob Coleman!" came a cry from the woods.

Keeping to the shadows, Kirk quartered toward the spot of white. It was Coleman's white bandage he had spotted, stained now. Coleman was sprawled over a deadfall, breathing heavily.

"I was going up to the Rim tomorrow and have another look for you," Kirk said. "Where's your horse?"

"I tried to get through the pass today," Coleman said.

He was gasping for breath. "Si Oldcamp shot the horse. I made it down here afoot." The man was spent.

"Think they followed you?"

Coleman shook his head. Kirk helped him into the house. He did not light a lamp, but stirred up the fire in the stove and put on coffee to boil.

"Ran into Hoskins yesterday," Coleman said. "He told me you bought this place. So I came down."

"Hoskins could have let you have a horse."

Coleman hugged his bad shoulder. "He turned me down. Said he didn't want trouble with Havenrite."

"I'll get you out of here, Bob," Kirk said. "Where's another pass besides the one at the Rim?"

Kirk made a sound of disgust when Coleman said the nearest alternate exit was sixty miles across the valley at Alder Gap.

"I've bought myself a ranch in a valley with only two exits," Kirk said grimly. "Hell, the pool's got no chance. All Havenrite has to do is bottle up both passes. We'll never get a pool cow out of the mountains. And if we can't sell beef, we'll starve."

"I could've told you that," Coleman said.

"If we can't get you out of the valley," Kirk said, "you can at least hang out at Larnet's Store. Havenrite won't try to touch you there."

Coleman shook his head. "Too many of the pool crowd will have it in for me because I worked for Beartrack."

"You're on our side of the fence now," Kirk reminded him.

"You got to remember this, Fallon," Coleman said. "I'm for the big outfits. I got no use for shirttail ranching. A man can't win at it and he's loco to try."

"Did you try it once?"

"My pa did. It killed my mother, and my sister was so old for her age from hard work that nobody would marry her. They're all gone now and it's a shame." Coleman sighed. "Pa could've gone to a town and opened a barbershop. He was a good barber, but somebody once hit him in the butt with a saddle rope and he thought he was a cowman."

"They say that about Sam Berryman," Kirk said.

"There's a difference," Bob Coleman told him. "Berryman got his start with a hundred thousand dollars of his daughter's money."

Kirk whistled in surprise. "That much?"

"Most of it's gone now," Coleman said. "Berryman had to have the best of everything. Last year he paid twenty thousand dollars for some blooded bulls. They died on him. Somebody sold him sick bulls. The poor fool." Coleman drank the coffee Kirk poured. "Much as I hate Havenrite's guts, if it wasn't for him, Beartrack would be to the wall by now."

"If I can't get you through the pass," Kirk said grimly, "you're going to have to make up your mind whose side you're on."

"I was Beartrack a hundred per cent till the other night. But Havenrite went too far. I wouldn't stand still for what he done."

"I don't think he'd have hanged Libby."

"Maybe not, but after he finished with you and Purley, he'd have let his crew have her."

The sat in the darkness, and Kirk clenched his fists. "I didn't think a man could be that low."

"You don't know Rex," Coleman said with a shake of his head. "He's a good cowman, and if anybody can save Beartrack, he can. But don't ever cross him. Man or woman, he'll make 'em pay."

"And I guess he figures Libby Squires crossed him by refusing to play second fiddle to the Berryman girl."

Kirk stepped to the door, peered out into the yard. The moon was climbing and threw a pale-yellow glow over the canyon. He heard no suspicious sounds.

"If you won't go to Larnet's, then I'll ride you down to El Cobre," Kirk said. "The doc can take a look at that shoulder."

"I'd rather take the chance of losing my arm than let Havenrite get to me."

Kirk felt a rising impatience. "What if those Beartrack boys from the Rim come down here? You can't just sit here."

"I doubt if they'll come this far," Coleman said. "They got to go by the Hoskins place to get here. I don't think the old man and his boys will put up with Beartrack ridin' over their land."

Kirk said, "I've got a hunch Hoskins is about ready to sell out to Havenrite."

"The hell you say! What was that?"

The sound came again, pebbles dropping against the

roof. And he knew that somebody was on the ledge above the back of the house.

"Fallon!" came a harsh voice. "You got one minute to walk out with your hands up. Bring Coleman with you. If you ain't out by then, we'll burn you out!"

"That was Si Oldcamp," Coleman groaned. "They did follow me here, damn 'em." He raised his voice. "Oldcamp, this is Bob. I always treated you right. Why don't you pull out and let us alone?"

"Sorry, Bob, but we're gettin' a bonus for this one. Havenrite rode up to the Rim a while ago. We'll split up a nice piece of money for this business. You two come on out!"

Coleman was desperately stalling for time. "How'd you know where to find me?"

"Old Man Hoskins said you'd likely come here to get a horse!"

"Havenrite will kill me," Coleman said loudly, "so what's the difference whether I die in here or outside?"

"Havenrite wants Fallon a lot more'n he wants you, Bob. Maybe there's a chance for you if you come out!"

"Go to hell!" Coleman shouted.

A shot crashed and the floor was sprayed with window glass.

From the wall where he had flattened himself, Kirk peered through a corner of the broken window. He counted six or seven shadows near the aspens. Likely there was one man or two on the ledge behind the house. He looked across the dark room, unable to see anything of Coleman save the white bandage.

"Looks like Havenrite has sewn us in the sack," Kirk said.

"You name it, Fallon," Coleman said hoarsely, "and I'll follow you."

Another shot crashed through the window, and the trees beyond the house were suddenly filled with winking red eyes. Both men flung themselves to the floor as bullets slammed through timbers and jarred the big table and went screaming off the stove.

Inching to the window when the firing eased off, Kirk fired at a shadow and a man yelped with pain. Something thudded against the roof; there was a sudden bloom of light in the house. He knew a torch had been flung against the tar-paper roof.

Flames crackled on the dry roof, began eating into the west wall. The wind had come up, and sparks swirled through the broken window.

In the passing moments the heat became intense. Outside there were shouts of "Watch the door! Get 'em when they come out!"

The flames roared; in the corral the dun went crazy. Kirk pushed Coleman across the room.

Kirk unbarred the rear door. "We'll make 'em think we're going out the front. Run for those rocks out back, soon as I open the front door!"

Bounding across the room, Kirk jerked open the front door and flung a chair across the porch.

"Here they come!" a man yelled, and the grove was alive again with the winking red eyes. Bullets slammed into the chair skittering across the yard.

Coleman was already out the back door, running for the shelter of the large rocks under the ledge. A few seconds later Kirk emerged. Somebody shouted from the ledge. A rifle cracked down on them. Kirk fired at the flash. There was a scream.

He saw Coleman running up ahead, bent over. Coleman faltered.

"Run, Bob, run!" Kirk shouted.

The back of Kirk's neck was wet as he sprinted. Any second he expected to feel the smash of a bullet from the rifle on the ledge.

He saw Coleman go down. A gun flashed almost in Kirk's face and he heard the vicious snarl of the bullet past his head. Half blinded by the gun flash, he fired at a shadowy figure. The shadow went down. Another streak of flame reached Coleman from the ridge. Coleman, who had been crawling on hands and knees toward the rocks, suddenly flattened out on the ground. He didn't move again.

Kirk fired at the ledge. A man scrambled to his feet and began to run. It was noon-bright in the yard now as the whole house erupted in flame. Embers, caught by the wind, made odd patterns against the night sky.

There was yelling from the front yard, where most of the Beartrack men were gathered. They started for the rocks where Kirk was holed up. Kirk shot at a running figure, missed. He tried to grab the prostrate Coleman by an arm and pull him to the comparative safety of the rocks.

Another shot cut from a thicket and Kirk jerked back his hand. It was light enough so he could see the back of Coleman's head. And he knew the man had no need for shelter now.

Si Oldcamp was crying, "Hank, Hank Ogden! Fallon's in the rocks. He must've got Lew, up on the ledge. Get another man up there!"

Kirk fired at the sound of Oldcamp's voice. The man broke off, cursing.

Kirk's mouth was dry and he was aware of the wild beating of his pulse. For a moment the firing let up. The entire house was a roaring mass of flames now. The roof fell in with a crash, sending a shower of sparks into the air. Kirk, crouching behind the boulder, held his fire. There was no use in wasting ammunition. He could hear them moving in the aspens, talking in low tones.

Kirk cocked his head and could hear a man moving up on the ledge, some twenty feet above. The cliff was undercut where he was making his stand. He was safe from the gunman above unless he leaned too far out and thus exposed himself. Carefully Kirk tilted his head and from a corner of his eye watched the ledge.

"Coleman's dead!" the man on the ledge shouted to his companions in the yard. "I can see him from up here!"

"Where's Fallon?" Oldcamp cried from somewhere near the barn.

"Below me somewheres!"

Kirk waited. He could hear another man scrambling up the ledge, then a murmur of voices. There were at least two men up there now, possibly three. Kirk was drenched with perspiration; it seeped, stinging, into the cuts opened by Jed Purley's fists.

He was about to gamble. If he could sprint to the west end of the yard, he might be able to make the tangle of buckbrush there before they cut him down. Then he caught sight of movement above. A man was leaning out over the ledge, trying to spot him. Kirk fired. There was the shrill cry of a man in pain. Then a shadow soared out from the ledge like a great bird, and came plunging down. It landed with a dull crash on the rocks some feet away.

The firing started up again from the grove. Bullets slammed into the rocks. Some of the more venturesome tried to run across the firelit yard. Kirk drove them back. An intense rage worked in him as he saw the fire consume the last of his house. It had been only a shack, but it had been the first place he had ever owned in his life.

There was a sudden shout from the trees to the south of the road. "What's goin' on there?"

Kirk, recognizing the voice, called, "Larnet, watch it! Beartrack out there!"

There was a burst of firing from Larnet's position, answering shots from the Beartrack men on the other side of the road.

"How many Beartrack, Fallon?" Larnet shouted, when the firing had tapered off again.

"Maybe ten!"

"We're twenty!" Larnet yelled back. "We'll do some hanging tonight when we catch 'em!"

"Careful, Larnet," Kirk called. "They're still out there!"

There was the sound of men running. Horses squealed and drove off into the brush with a crash of hoofs.

From some distance away Hank Ogden's voice came clearly. "We'll get you, Fallon! There'll be another day!"

Kirk listened to the sounds of their passing. A splatter of gunshots sped them on their way.

Kirk waited five minutes, until he was sure the Beartrack men had gone. Then he cautiously emerged from the rocks and spoke Larnet's name. Larnet and six pool men came walking up from the trees, carrying their rifles.

"You ran a good bluff on them," Kirk said, wiping his face with a soiled bandanna.

"Never reveal your strength to the enemy," Larnet said gravely. "I learned that in the war." He looked at the ruins of Kirk's house; the fire was a dull glow in the yard. "We were on our way to see you when we saw the fire. We figured you ought to know that all hell's goin' to bust loose. Hoskins sold out to Rex Havenrite."

Kirk sank down on a rock, staring dully at the fire. He jacked out the empties from his revolver, loaded it mechanically. His mind was dull. He ached, and he felt bitter.

One of the pool men had been scouting around the yard. "You got two of 'em, Fallon," the man called. "Good shooting!"

Suddenly Kirk was sick of it. They spoke of shooting men as they would deer. "Nice shooting," the man had said to him.

"I've got a quit-claim deed to this place. I'll sign it over for a thousand dollars."

The men looked at him as if he had lost his senses.

Larnet said, "There isn't a thousand dollars cash on the mountain."

"Five hundred," Kirk said.

This created a stir, and some of the men began talking between themselves.

"The game getting too rough for you, Fallon?" Larnet asked. And when Kirk didn't reply, he went on, "The Shatto brothers are dead because of you. Jed Purley's gone over to the other side because of you."

Kirk ran a trembling hand over his jaw. No matter how senseless this fight seemed to be, he did owe these men something. If they hadn't come up here when they did, he would have been killed before the sun came up.

"You're worried that if this thing keeps on, you may get euchered into a spot where you'll be forced to kill Sam Berryman," Larnet said. "And you know the girl would hate you for it." Larnet shrugged. "You've got a stake in this, Fallon. That's all I was pointing out. Don't quit on us now."

"So Hoskins sold out."

"That means Havenrite has got us in the middle," Larnet said. "He can start squeezing us any time he feels like it."

Kirk looked at the bald storekeeper, standing with the other men near the ruins of the porch.

"If Beartrack tries to move onto any pool ranch," Kirk said, "will you fight? If they take one pool cow, will you go after it? Instead of waiting till they sell their beef and then steal the money? That makes you outlaws. But there's no law in the world says a man can't cut his own beef out of a herd."

"Easy for you to talk," one of the men grumbled. "You ain't got a wife and kids."

"So that's it," Kirk said, his mouth tightening. "You let a few hotheads like Yañez and Purley do the dirty work, while you sit back and worry. No wonder Havenrite thinks he can run you out."

Larnet said quietly, "When the time comes, we'll fight." He sighed. "Guess we better bury the dead."

"Start with Bob Coleman," Kirk said. "He's the only one of that bunch who deserves a decent grave."

"So they got him," Larnet said, and shook his head sadly.

One of the men said, "Wonder who'll tell Si Oldcamp's wife."

"Don't worry, she'll know about it soon enough," Larnet said.

Kirk felt something clutch at his throat. Another one, he thought. First Irma Shatto and now this Oldcamp woman. "A great country for widows," he said bitterly, and led the way to an outbuilding where shovels were stored.

Chapter Fifteen

SAM BERRYMAN awoke with a terrible pounding in his head and an old familiar taste in his mouth. On a table beside the large carved oak bedstead was a bottle with a thumb and forefinger width of whisky left in it. He drank it all and shuddered. He sat up in the bed, a narrow-shouldered, gray-haired man.

There was a light rap of knuckles on the door and it started to open. "Dad—"

He made a frantic effort to hide the bottle, but it slipped from his trembling hands and skated across the rug. Vanessa, wearing a brown dress, a string of red beads about her throat, picked up the bottle and set it back on the table. Then she gathered her skirts and sat down on the edge of the bed. She looked at him severely, and he refused to meet her eyes.

"Was I—I mean, did I make a fool of myself in front of the guests?" he managed to say. His throat was dry and sweat dampened his shirt. He had slept in his clothes.

"Only once before since I've come to live with you has this happened," she said.

"That was when I woke up to the fact that I was a fool to buy Beartrack with no water to speak of on it."

"And what's the excuse this time, Dad?" She had folded her hands in her lap. When he did not immediately answer her, she said, "Is it because of Kirk Fallon?"

He nodded.

"You couldn't face him here yesterday, so you got drunk."

He stared out the window at a wind devil kicking up a funnel of dust.

Vanessa said, "Did you tell me the truth about what happened in Chihuahua?"

"God's truth. It was the Comanches."

"And yet you ran and left him. What if the Indians had returned? They would have killed him."

"I've told you," he said, his thin body shuddering. "I thought Kirk was dead."

"I'm going to tell Rex to gather enough cattle and sell them so we can realize seventy-eight hundred dollars in cash."

He looked at her in surprise. "But we can't. We have no market but the fort. And if we try to drive north out of the valley, the pool can ambush us."

"That's what Rex has told you, but I'm beginning to wonder just how badly the pool hates us. They seemed friendly enough yesterday, for the most part. I think there can be peace here. I'm going to work for it, Dad."

"You can't win. Just like yesterday, Fallon and Purley fighting over that woman—"

"It was Purley's idea, not Fallon's."

"Sticking up for him?" Berryman shot at her.

"I think Rex put Jed Purley up to it. And—and Rex snatched a bottle out of your hand and threw it. He struck Fallon in the back and nearly ended the fight. My maid saw him do it. I—I've changed my mind about Rex Havenrite."

"Now you listen to me." He swung his thin legs over the edge of the bed. His trousers were stained from the whisky he had spilled on them. "Don't go against Rex. He's our only chance, honey. Let him work this thing out his own way."

She got to her feet, her mouth tight. "Dad, have you no backbone at all? Is that why Mother couldn't live with you? Is that why you drank every time you came home to see us? Was it because you were ashamed you weren't a man?"

There was a dead silence in the big room. Sunlight washing through the window was reflected in a mahogany-framed wall mirror, Berryman looked sick. Vanessa gave a little cry and dropped to her knees and took his thin moist hands in hers.

"Dad, I'm sorry. I shouldn't have said that. But—"

He sat frozen. "It's the truth," he said in a dead voice. "Like Rex told me once. I've got no guts."

"You've taken so much from him," she said. "You're a better man than he'll ever be. Don't take anything else from him. Ever."

They looked at each other for a long moment, the girl and the father she hardly knew. From the yard came the sound of an ax bit on wood, the neigh of horses, the barking of a dog. Some riders went quickly past the house and down through the trees toward the bunkhouse.

There were muffled shouts, and then a new sound, the wail of a woman. Quickly Vanessa rose to her feet. She stepped to the window and looked toward the quarters of the married riders, where a crowd had gathered. Men were running that way. The wailing continued, and the sound was a knife cutting into her heart.

"There's been trouble of some sort," she said, and felt a terrible apprehension. "I'll go and see what it is." She hurried out of the house.

She pushed her way through the crowd gathered in front of the one-story stone building that had been cut up into small living quarters. A brown-haired, homely woman was standing rigid in front of one of the doors, the knuckles of her right hand grinding against her teeth. As she screamed, the men stood around uncertainly. Two other wives came running up and tried to take her by the arms, but in a frenzy she shook them off.

"What is it, Mrs. Oldcamp?" Vanessa demanded.

"It's Si!" Then the woman's wild gaze centered on Vanessa. She pointed a forefinger; the knuckles were bleeding where her teeth had bit through the skin. "You—you! Had 'em down here, waltzin' and feedin' 'em and them drinkin' your whisky. And you struttin' in your silk an' all the time they was plannin' to kill Si!"

"Kill?" Vanessa was stunned.

Hank Ogden shoved his squat figure through the press of riders in front of the building. He removed his hat. His hair was black, matted with sweat. His beard was ragged. "There's been bad trouble, Miss Berryman. We just rode in and I was aimin' to tell Havenrite and your pa."

"What's happened?" Vanessa's lips seemed frozen.

"Kirk Fallon killed Bob Coleman. And when we went down to get him, he killed Si Oldcamp and Joe Beavers."

"Oh, my God!" Vanessa cried. The Oldcamp woman screeched at her insanely until the other two women forceably dragged her into the building.

With the riders watching her, Vanessa walked slowly back toward the house, her feet dragging. Her heart weighed a ton. She heard somebody running up behind her, but did not look around.

Rex Havenrite caught her lightly by the arm. "Never

you mind, we'll finish this. Fallon is a killer. You can see that now. I'll take some men and go and get him."

"This is the excuse you need, isn't it, Rex?"

"I'm sorry, Vanessa. I know you kind of liked him. But I could have told you all along the kind he is."

She stood looking up into the amber eyes a moment, and then she said through her teeth, "Rex Havenrite, you're a liar!"

"Wait a minute, now!" His face turned red with sudden rage.

"This is a put-up job. I know it is! I'm going to tell Fallon."

With half the crew looking on, Havenrite made a grab for her, but missed as Vanessa, hiking up her skirts around her long legs, dashed for the house. For a moment Havenrite seemed undecided. Then he took off after her.

He caught her in the main hall and she crashed her open hand against his nose. Roaring with pain, he got her wrists. She kicked him and got a hand free and raked her nails down the side of his face. Four bloodied tracks instantly appeared on his cheek. She ran.

With a cry of rage he lunged after her. He caught her by the ends of her long hair and spun her against the wall with such force that she was momentarily stunned. He tried to pin her there with his arms, but she slipped away. He was after her again as she reached the doorway at the end of the hall. He tore her hand from the knob. As she screamed he struck her across the mouth. She pitched to the floor, senseless.

He knelt down, cradled her head in his lap. "Vanessa, Vanessa. I didn't mean it. But you get me so riled." Her eyes opened slowly. "Don't cross me again," he warned. "I know what's best for both of us. You leave me handle things."

She stared at him dazedly. Her lower lip was cut and bleeding. Her black hair hung loosely about her shoulders.

He was aware then that the door at the end of the hall had been opened. Sam Berryman stood there, wearing a wrinkled gray suit. He was in his sock feet. Havenrite looked up from where he knelt on the floor, wary now. He let Vanessa's head slip back to the floor. He didn't know how long Berryman had been standing there. The man's face was white, and there were dark shadows under the eyes. But in the eyes themselves was something Havenrite had never seen there before. A terrible wildness. Berryman held a .32 revolver, and the hammer was back.

Slowly Havenrite got to his feet. "Look, Sam, I didn't mean to hit her. But she went a little loco."

Vanessa was stirring on the floor, wiping numbly at the blood on her mouth.

Berryman said, "Get away from him, Vannie." He had not called her that since she was a little girl. "This is something I should've done a long time ago."

He was still half drunk, a man in the grip of an emotion that shook his whole narrow body. He was still speaking when Havenrite's gun crashed. Berryman staggered and looked foolishly down at the cocked revolver in his own hand. He sagged down to the floor. His sock feet stirred a few times and then he was still.

Dazed, Vanessa brushed dark hair from her eyes. She sat on the fine oaken floor, her back to the wall. She stared at her father, and the blood seeping out from under the linen shirt she had bought him last year on a trip to Denver.

There was no screaming left in her; no tears.

She could hear servants in the back part of the house calling excitedly to one another.

Havenrite holstered his gun. He seemed shaken, but his ruthless drive prevented any show of remorse.

"He put a gun on me. You saw that. He was drunk and I had to protect myself." He straightened his heavy shoulders. "I love you, Vanessa. I mean it. I'm sorry I shot him. But it's not going to make any difference to us. You understand?" he whirled for the door. "I'll be back by tomorrow night."

He stormed out into the yard and waved back the men who were running toward the house, drawn by the screams and the shot.

"Saddle up!" he roared at them. "Every Beartrack man on the place. We're going to finish this!"

Vanessa recovered from her shock and followed the Mexican servant who carried her father into the back part of the house. The man put Berryman on the bed. When she saw her father lying pale and unmoving in the center of his big hand-carved bed, she was struck by his slight stature. To her he had always seemed to be a much larger man.

Vanessa shook her head to clear it. She looked at the servants, standing wide-eyed along the wall, gazing at the *patrón* with blood all over his chest.

"One of you ride to town for the doctor," she ordered, and then rushed to a closet where she kept her linens. She tore up a white sheet. "Let him live," she prayed. "Let him live. For I believe he has found himself at last."

On the bed Sam Berryman fought against great waves of heat and pain. "They've got Ruben!" he cried, rising from the bed, his eyes wild. "I saw what they did to Ruben! Don't let them do it to me!"

She tried to silence him so he could save his strength, but the wildness did not leave his eyes. He screamed a story that had been buried for years in some remote cavern of his mind. A story of a gold trek to California in the late forties; an attack by Piutes, and their gruesome manner of discouraging the whites from violating their homeland. She listened to it, and felt a great pity for this man.

The story was told and Sam Berryman sank back upon the bed, his face shining with perspiration. He had a smile for his daughter and then closed his eyes.

She felt for his pulse. There was none.

Chapter Sixteen

IT WAS NEARLY NOON when Libby Squires came to Larnet's Store. She hurried to Kirk, her green eyes concerned. "I'm sorry about your house, Kirk." She wore her blue shirt and Levis. Her auburn hair was in braids. "I saw the flames last night. Some of the boys came by and told me what happened." She gave him a pensive look. "I waited until daylight for you to come by."

He said, "Remember what I told you yesterday? Purley's in love with you."

Her face changed. "And you're not." She gave a small laugh. "You're the first man I ever chased, Fallon. It's usually the other way around. It seems I can never get myself a husband."

"What about Purley?"

"I told him I wouldn't marry a thief," she said.

He shrugged and looked out the doorway at the yard, touched by the noon sun. In the distance he could see the smudge that marked the site of El Cobre, far down in the valley.

Not too long ago he had cursed the Shatto place, calling himself a fool for buying it. But now the loss of the house seemed important. He felt he was at loose ends again, and the urge came to abandon everything and ride out, and to hell with the money he had paid for the place. But he knew he could not go. He had something to settle. Something of as great importance as the business with Berryman. Bob Coleman had saved his life the other night. And when Bob Coleman had come to him for help, he had been murdered by the Beartrack men. And they had been sent by Havenrite. Kill two birds with the same stone, Havenrite had probably said. Follow Coleman to Fallon's place and then finish them both and make it appear as if they had shot it out.

Larnet, looking out the front window, said, "Here comes Jed Purley, damn his soul."

There came the sounds of a fast-moving horse. There were half a dozen other pool men in the store. They moved to the windows with Kirk and Libby to watch Purley spur his horse across the clearing. The big man flung himself off and came pounding up the steps.

When he saw Kirk, he halted on the porch, his body stiffened, head thrown back.

Ray Larnet said, "You ain't welcome in my store, Purley."

Purley flushed, then seemed to let the tension run out of him. "All right,' he said, "if that's the way you feel. I don't give a hang about the rest of you. But I don't want to see Libby hurt."

Larnet gave Purley a narrow-eyed look. "What's up, Jed?"

"I was heading for El Cobre when I saw Havenrite come along the Beartrack road with the whole Beartrack crew. Must be twenty-five men. They're heading this way."

Libby said coolly, "I can take care of myself, Jed. I always have. But thanks for the warning." She turned to look at the pool men on the wide veranda. "What do we do now?"

They had grown pale, all except Kirk Fallon. He was staring south along the El Cobre road, where it twisted throught the trees.

Purley touched Libby on the arm. "You've got a ranch and Beartrack will hit you like everybody else."

Dalmyre, who ranched behind Old Man Hoskins, looked grim. "This might be some kind of trick." He glared at Purley. "The other night Havenrite was goin' to put a rope around Purley's neck. Then the next thing we know Purley is drinkin' Havenrite's whisky."

Purley gave Kirk Fallon a long look. "I reckon everybody knows why I acted the damn fool. A jealous man ain't responsible."

"You don't have to be jealous any longer," Kirk said. "If I've got any luck left at all, I'm going to marry Vanessa Berryman."

They all looked at him in surprise. He felt completely foolish once the words were out. It had been a spontaneous utterance. And he was baffled as to why he had suddenly give voice to a thought that at best had only been a faint hope.

Libby Squires was watching his face; now she looked

away. "You'd have more chance walking barefoot through cactus than you've got of marrying her." She seemed angered. She turned and looked at the others. "I'm glad Jed's come back to our side. How about you?"

There was a shuffling of feet on the porch; some of them were reluctant to forgive Purley.

Kirk said, "I'm glad he's back."

Purley looked at him in surprise.

Dalmyre cleared his throat. "Old Man Hoskins has sold out and that leaves us on the limb. And the Shatto brothers are gone and Havenrite is headin' this way. A bit ago Libby said Fallon had about as much chance of putting a ring on Vanessa Berryman's finger as he had of walking barefoot through cactus. Well, that's more of a chance than we got of fightin' Beartrack."

Kirk Fallon looked at the rancher. "You're giving up then?"

"They can burn you out and try to frame Coleman's murder on you, Fallon," Dalmyre said. "And that's one thing. You're alone. You got nobody to worry about but you."

Kirk said, "I've seen it happen before. The shirttail outfits talk until the showdown. Then they either pull out or let somebody else carry the fight for them."

"You know how much Hoskins got for his place?" Dalmyre demanded. "Two thousand dollars. And he's got the best place in the mountains. He was glad to get it. He said two thousand cash was better than a three-by-six hole in the ground."

"There's a word in the dictionary," Kirk said. "It's fight. F-I-G-H-T." He surveyed the grim men.

One of them said, "Easy for you to talk. You've done plenty of killin' in your time. I ain't shot nothin' but game."

Kirk lifted his hands, let them fall. He couldn't blame these men. Most of them had come here after the war, taken up land and tried to make a go of ranching. But the business had outgrown them. It wasn't a case of running a few head of beef; you had to run them in the thousands. One day the railroad would be here, and then the little outfits could have a reasonably close market. But until then the drives of hundreds of miles were not profitable unless a sizable herd could be sent to rail's end. And there wasn't enough cattle in the whole Juniper Pool to make an average-sized cattle drive.

Kirk shrugged. "You might as well go home and pack your wagons and pull out. If Havenrite has got the Hoskins place, it's only a matter of time until he pressures the rest of you to abandon your places."

Ray Larnet took a hitch at his pants. "He won't make me give up my store. That's for sure."

There was a faint sound of horses in the distance, and the men on the porch froze and peered in the direction of El Cobre. They could see a band of horsemen moving up.

Kirk went into the store, where he had spent the night, and picked up his rifle. "One thing we Yanks learned in the war, and that's what helped lick the Johnnies. An unhorsed cavalry isn't worth a damn. A horse makes a sight broader target than a man."

"I hate to shoot a horse," Larnet said gravely. He shot a worried glance in the direction of the riders, about a half mile down the road.

"You can't worry very much if it's a choice between your neck or a horse's life." Kirk started down the steps. When none of them followed, he looked back. "We could put Havenrite's men on the seats of their pants if we acted quick."

Dalmyre said, "It's all right for you to talk big, Fallon. But it's your comin' here that's brought all this to a head. Maybe we could've stuck it out a little longer up here, till we could maybe get word to the governor and have a U.S. marshal sent here. But no, you had to come and try to collect a bill you thought Berryman owed you. And you killed Pete and Charlie Shatto."

"I'm with you, Fallon," Jed Purley said, and came to stand by his side. "Yesterday I hated your insides. But you had a chance to dump me headfirst into one of them barbecue pits, and you didn't do it. Maybe I still don't like you worth a damn, but I'll side you."

Larnet came down the stairs and three others followed. Libby came to stand at Kirk's side.

Kirk looked around. "Six men and a woman," he said, "against twenty-five." He looked at the seven ranchers and their hands left on the porch. He said harshly to Jed Purley, "You must want to get your head shot off almighty bad. Personally, I'm not damn fool enough to commit suicide."

He moved to his horse.

"Where you going?" Larnet demanded.

"Wave the white flag when Havenrite comes over the hill," Kirk said. "Likely he'll talk a spell before he starts shooting." He looked at Libby, standing beside Jed Purley. Purley still bore the marks of Kirk's fists.

There was no expression on Libby's face as he rode out.

He had gone but a hundred yards from the store when he heard a shout from the advancing Beartrack men. About a dozen of them peeled off from the main body and came after him at a hard run. But he had a fresh horse, and by the time he had climbed through the timber, crossed a ridge, and doubled back over a high mesa, he had lost them.

He dismounted, loosened the cinch, and let the dun blow. He listened attentively, but there was no sound of firing brought to him on the mountain breeze.

There was one chance he could help Vanessa and those fools in the mountains, and he decided to take the gamble. He might meet with a rebuff, but it was worth a try.

He cut down out of the mountains and at last hit the El Cobre road. The sky was very clear save for thunderheads building up over the peaks across the valley. Whenever he saw a dust cloud he pulled off into the timber. But he met no Beartrack riders..

He remembered how, at the close of the war, he had taken part in a discussion of strategy. It was agreed that if Lee could be captured or killed, the will to continue the struggle would be lost to the South. One man held the South together. Not Jeff Davis, but Lee.

It was the same with Beartrack, he thought, as he loped toward El Cobre. The only threat against the rest of the country was Havenrite. It he were eliminated, the threat would be gone.

Having made his decision, he quickened his pace.

When he saw a solitary rider coming toward him from the Beartrack road, he grew wary. It was Vanessa, and she wore the same black riding clothes that she had worn the day she found him at Libby's place. When she saw him she pulled up and dismounted. She stood looking at him, her face pale, her eyes wide with shock.

Slowly he swung down. "What's the matter?" was all he could think to say. She looked so pathetic, so frightened.

"When it happened all I could think of was you. I had to find you, Kirk. I was coming to your place."

He came closer, saw that her mouth was swollen. He felt a terrible rage. "Somebody hit you!"

She seemed not to hear. "Dad—he died."

"Died?"

"Rex shot him."

"But why? How?"

"Rex hit me and Dad had a gun and— Well, he never had a chance to use it." Her bruised mouth quivered, and tears glistened in her eyes.

"Why did he hit you?"

"It was because of what happened at your place last night. Rex said you had killed Bob Coleman and another man. And I didn't believe him and he chased me and I clawed his face and he knocked me down."

Kirk's jaw hardened and he felt an empty sensation in the pit of his stomach. How many men had died, how much trouble had been caused by his coming to this country?

She clung to him now, and he supported her weight by holding her about the waist. "I wanted to find you," she murmured. "To explain about Dad."

"Don't talk," he said. "We'll go to town."

She shook her black head and he could feel the silky texture of her hair beneath his chin. "After Dad was shot, he talked a lot about things I never knew. He had an older brother named Ruben. My uncle. And once when Dad was younger they started for California with some men to hunt gold. And one of the men—" She broke off and looked up at him. "One of the men found an Indian girl out alone. And that night the Piutes attacked their camp. Dad was the only one who escaped. But before he got away he saw what they did to his brother and the others. It haunted him. That's why—" She began to cry softly.

"You mean in Mexico. The Comanches that hit our ranch."

"He was frenized with fear," she sobbed. "He— Can a man be afraid of something and still not be a coward?"

"Every man has something he fears."

"But not you," she said, and she got him by the arms and shook him and peered anxiously up into his face. "It's what has made me think of you so much lately. Your lack of fear."

"You don't know," he said bitterly.

"You faced Jed Purley and you whipped him."

"Purley was nothing to face. He was mad—crazed by jealously. A man doesn't use his head when he's upset. Maybe next time Purley would be the lucky one."

"You're not afraid of Rex," she said, drawing back a little. "You struck him that night in my room. You fought them all and they said you were a tough man. All except Rex. He's the one who hit you over the head when your back was turned."

"Is there anywhere in town you can stay? Where Havenrite can't find you?"

"The Oberleys'. Mrs. Oberley has been nice to me." She wiped her eyes on the sleeve of her black shirt. "You're not afraid of anything. Tell me you're not."

"Why is it so important?"

"I've got to know that there's somebody good—somebody decent left in the world. Somebody not afraid. If you're afraid of Rex, then it means that his kind of man will rule this country. And there will be no goodness left." She closed her eyes a moment. "Tell me you're not afraid."

He looked toward the mountains, washed golden by the westering sun. "I'm as much afraid as your father was."

"But of what?"

"Of becoming the sort of man Havenrite is."

"Not you. You could never be his kind."

"These things I've done grow on a man," he said slowly. "Five years I had but a single aim—find your father. I sold my gun to a lot of men and I wore a badge at times. I found a certain release from pressure when there was trouble. Those things become easier and easier. I killed Pete Shatto and his brother. And last night I killed two of your Beartrack men."

"Kirk, don't—"

"They were attacking my place, sure. But the killing becomes a habit. You kill one more man, then another. And one day you're no longer burdened by a conscience."

"But you have a conscience, Kirk. When you first came to this country I was afraid for my father's life. But even though you felt justified, maybe, you didn't kill him."

She tipped her forehead against his chest. He looked down at the glossy head, the black hair carefully parted and drawn back. He put his hand on her shoulder and felt its softness.

"I understand this country now," she said without looking up. "I understand that you cannot reason with a man like Rex. You—" Her voice caught. "Kirk, I want you to kill him."

He was silent, and withdrew his hand from her shoulder. He looked toward town, where a blue haze from charcoal fires lay over the flat roofs. A freighter lumbered downgrade from beyond El Cobre, chain-locked rear wheels sending up gouts of yellow dust.

"I want you to kill him, Kirk. I never wanted a man to die before."

"Your father shouldn't have put a gun on him."

"Are you defending Rex?"

His mouth hardened. "Your father let Havenrite take over. Your father was responsible for dead men and much misery."

"It was Rex, not my father, that was responsible."

"Your father sanctioned it. Then he puts a gun on a man he knows to be dangerous. Because his daughter has been struck in the mouth by this man."

"Wouldn't you do as much?"

"If it had been my daughter," Kirk said coldly, "she would never have got close enough for Havenrite ever to put a hand on her."

"You blame my father for everything."

"You've got friends in Santa Fe. Go to them. Maybe in a month things will be changed so that you can come back."

"If there's anything to come back to," she said bitterly, and gave him a long look out of her swollen eyes. "I think I dislike you very much."

"I'll ride you to the Oberley place. Have them buy you a ticket to Santa Fe."

"Why don't you want me here?"

"Because I have one thing to concentrate on. I don't want you around." His voice was rough.

"I'm not going to the Oberley place," she said.

"You are. Point out the house."

"No."

"I'm tired of fooling with you." He caught her around the waist and swung her up into the saddle of her black horse.

Then they rode. She did not speak to him until they drew up in front of a two-story white house a block from the business district.

"What are you going to do?" she demanded hoarsely.

"I've got a ranch in the mountains. For better or for worse, it's mine. I'm not giving it up."

He rode, a tall man, toward the main street.

She watched him, biting her bruised lips. And at last she went up the porch steps and knocked on the door. A plump woman wearing a gray dress put an arm about her waist and led her into the house.

Chapter Seventeen

AT THE LIVERY Kirk turned his horse over to a lank, squint-eyed stableman. "Is Bert Wingate in town?" Kirk asked.

"Down at Oberley's. Come in last night. I hear hell is bustin' loose up there." He flung a thin hand toward the mountains.

"Where'd you hear that?" Kirk demanded.

"Doc Graham. He went out to Beartrack to tend Sam Berryman. Seen the whole Beartrack crew headin' for the mountains. Goin' to be trouble. Well, them ragged-pants boys up there oughta know by this time they can't buck the big outfits. Bert Wingate tried to tell 'em that ten years ago, when they first moved up there." The stableman spat and added, "I guess you heard that Sam Berryman's dead."

"I heard," Kirk said, and, carrying his rifle, moved to the wide doorway where shadows were thickening across the runway.

"News sure gets around," the stableman said. "Berryman didn't know a damn thing about the cow business, but I liked drinkin' his whisky down at Oberley's."

Kirk turned and surveyed the lank man coldly. "I've seen some mighty smart cowmen go broke. A good market and plenty of water sometimes counts for more than savvy."

"Hell, Fallon, I thought you hated Berryman."

Without replying Kirk walked out.

Oberley's was fairly crowded. Oberley, behind his bar, his sparse hair neatly parted, said, "What's this I hear about you shooting Bob Coleman?"

"What about it?" Kirk demanded.

"If it's true, you're not welcome here, Fallon," the saloonman said.

"I didn't kill him. Bob was hiding out at my place when Beartrack jumped him." He looked around the big room with its beamed ceiling and cracked adobe walls. "I don't see any tears being shed. Or maybe you haven't heard about Sam Berryman."

"We heard," Oberley said, and rubbed his jaw. "But we never had much use for him. He spent all his daughter's money trying to be a big auger. You can't much pity a man like that."

Kirk spotted Bert Wingate at a poker table. "You made me a proposition once. Town marshal."

The small rancher put down the cards he had been holding and got to his feet. His eyes were hard under bushy white brows. "You could've had it, Fallon. And maybe had you taken that badge, some boys that are dead would be alive today."

Kirk felt his face getting red. "Things are different now."

"Yeah, some." Wingate expertly spat into a brass cuspidor by his table. "You say you didn't kill Coleman. Maybe not, but we're not sure. And maybe you had a right to shoot Oldcamp and Beavers to protect your property. But Oldcamp's widow rode in with Doc Graham, and I don't think you could convince her it was all right."

Kirk said, "What does a man do in this country? Throw up his hands because a big outfit like Beartrack blows a loud horn?"

Sam Wingate waved a small hand at the cards and the stacks of chips on the table. "You buy into a game like this, Fallon, and you play your cards as they fall."

"I play my own hand. I don't ask help."

"The hell you say, Fallon," Wingate said, his voice hardening. "I asked you to consider taking a badge. Because you've got a rep already made. I thought with you showing a little law in this town it would make Rex Havenrite think twice about gunning down those poor bastards up in the mountains. But no, you had to buy into the game your way. You picked up a ranch from a widow dirt cheap and—"

"I was trying to do the Shatto woman a favor."

"And also you done her a favor, I s'pose, by killin' her husband."

There was a shuffling of feet on the hard-packed dirt floor, a jingle of spurs. Men exchanged glances. Those at the bar put their backs to it and regarded Kirk with unfriendly eyes.

"All right," Kirk said to Wingate. "You don't like me,

and I'm beginning to change my mind about you. So let's put this on a business basis. What about that badge?"

"So far as I'm concerned, now that you've bought into the game your way, you can play it out. You've kicked Beartrack in the face by killing their men. And as much as I don't like the outfit, you can stand on your own two feet without a badge."

Kirk's gaze thinned. "You're a good rancher, Wingate. Have you got money enough to take Beartrack off Vanessa Berryman's hands?"

Wingate looked surprised. "Well, reckon so, but there's a few items you haven't thought of. Water—"

"The Shatto place is near enough to Beartrack. It's got water. I'll deed it over to you, if it'll help."

Wingate blinked his eyes. "I don't want your ranch. And even if I did, Rex Havenrite wouldn't set still and let me move in there. He's got a twenty-five-per-cent interest in Beartrack."

"That you can take up with his heirs, if any. Because I intend to hunt him down and kill him."

There was a heavy silence, during which men looked at each other.

Oberley set out a bottle and glass. "On the house, Fallon," he said. "I'm sorry I got tough with you about Bob Coleman."

Kirk did not touch the bottle. "The Berryman girl is with your wife. It might be the kind thing to do after her father's funeral to see that she gets on the stage for Santa Fe."

Before anyone could say anything he walked out, his rifle swinging from his long right arm, the brim of his hat tilted to keep the light of the fading sun out of his eyes.

Slowly he crossed the plaza to a cantina, and here he felt at home. He spoke Spanish and drank tequila. The Mexicans regarded him somberly. He stood at the end of the bar, his rifle against his knee. He kept watching the main street.

Nobody said anything in Oberley's for a full half minute after Kirk Fallon walked out. Then Oberley said, "I believe he means it."

"Meaning it and doing it are two different things," Bert Wingate said. "Havenrite might be mighty good with a gun, but he's not fool enough to face up to a man when he can let his crew do the job."

"Well, let's drink to Kirk Fallon," Oberley said. "Seeing as how he and Sam Berryman was partners once, it might be fitting to bury them at the same time."

Chapter Eighteen

LIBBY SQUIRES said, "Rex, now that you've killed Vanessa's father, she'll never marry you."

"It's the ranch, not Vanessa," Havenrite said, and gave her a bold look. "You and me. We might take up again, Lib. I always did have a fancy for you."

They were in front of Larnet's Store. The pool men were on the porch, looking self-conscious about the rifles they held. In the yard the Beartrack men were lounging in the shade.

Libby smiled with her teeth, and rubbed her throat. "I haven't forgotten the night you hanged Yáñez," she told Havenrite.

"Well, nothing would have happened to you. I only wanted to scare you."

"Honest, Rex?"

"Sure."

She smiled and bit her lip and seemed to debate. "Loyalties are so mixed up."

"We could go up to your place and talk it over," Havenrite suggested.

"Well, as long as everybody's going to be friends again," Libby said, "I guess it can't do any harm."

Jed Purley, standing on the porch, said, "Libby—" His face was tight with rage.

But Libby, down in the yard, turned her back on Jed Purley. She walked through the press of Beartrack men, hips swinging in her tight-fitting Levis. They watched her, as did Havenrite. She booted her rifle and mounted and rode slowly up the road that led to her ranch.

Jed Purley put down a hand for his gun, but Ray Larnet got both hands around his wrist. "Don't, Jed. Don't. She isn't worth it."

Purley seemed to come out of his daze. He looked at the storekeeper, then went down the steps to his horse.

When he was in the saddle, Havenrite said, "Where you going, Jed?"

"As far away as I can get."

He heard Havenrite's laughter as he rode into the aspens. Havenrite, with those four livid marks down the side of his face. Why was everybody afraid of Havenrite? He and Yáñez had been the only ones with guts enough to fight back. And now Yáñez was dead, hanged. Purley touched his throat. It had been close for him, too. And then like a fool he'd let Havenrite get him drunk at Oberley's and talk about fighting Kirk Fallon.

He thought of Libby. Well, he deserved to lose her. Libby had warned him about going after Beartrack money. He had to give her credit for being fair on that score, anyway. She said if he tried to steal beef money she was through with him. But he had thought he could talk her out of it.

But then Fallon had come along, and Libby wasn't interested any longer.

Purley halted deep in the trees, seeing that five Beartrack riders were coming leisurely along the road. And he sensed they were after him. Once they were out of sight of the store they would either shoot him or take him prisoner on Havenrite's orders.

And Havenrite had come up to the store today with his crew—those that hadn't taken off after Kirk Fallon. And Larnet and the rest of the pool had stood there and let Havenrite talk about being neighborly now that Berryman was dead. There was no use in fighting among themselves, Rex said.

But Jed and Larnet and some of the others knew that Havenrite was making concessions because he had been forced to kill Sam Berryman. Berryman wasn't Bob Coleman or Oldcamp or any of the regular crew. No, Berryman owned a big ranch and somebody might get the governor's ear and a U.S. marshal might show up here. Havenrite would then need the backing of as many friends as he could get. And the way the pool let him talk without answering him back showed, in Purley's judgment, that they would be afraid to do any complaining to a marshal. A marshal would come and go, but Havenrite and Beartrack would be around for a long time.

If they could be reasonably sure of being allowed to ranch in the mountains unmolested by Beartrack, the pool would probably let well enough alone. Short memories, Purley thought.

He let the five Beartrack men continue downgrade in the twilight. When they were out of sight of the store and hurried to catch up with him, they would find him gone.

Purley turned his horse in the direction of Libby Squires' place. He wondered now at his lack of jealousy. So she was that kind of woman. So it was better for a man to learn it now, before he married her. His place bordered hers and he had dreamed of consolidating the two places, and raising a family here in the mountains. Going to town once a month on Saturday, so the missus could buy yard goods and he could go to Oberley's and maybe risk a couple of dollars in a poker game, and drink a little. And brag about his kids.

A long-gone empty feeling was rooted in the pit of his stomach as he acknowledged the impossibility of this dream. He knew what the country thought of him. A brawler. A drinker. But he'd changed since he started going with Libby. Sure, he knew about Havenrite and her, and how Havenrite had turned her down when he saw a chance to marry Beartrack Ranch. And he knew Rex well enough to know the man would still marry Beartrack. He would force Vanessa Berryman to marry him.

Rex would think of something.

As he rode up through the thickening shadows, he thought of the Berryman girl. She was pretty, but she was too soft, and she didn't have Libby's eyes or her warm smile. Purley caught himself just as he was about to be knocked from the saddle by a low-hanging branch. He ducked just in time and vowed to quit his daydreaming. Hell, when a woman was gone, she was gone, wasn't she? He'd keep going on until he reached Nevada, maybe. Somebody might buy the ranch, such as it was, and send him the money. He'd buy some fancy clothes and live in Virginia City and drink good bourbon and be a gentleman. But this dream, he knew, was even more incongruous than the other. Him a gentleman!

You poor damn fool, Jed, he told himself.

Everybody thought he was stupid, and he probably was. His brains were mixed with too much bone. No wonder Libby turned from him to Fallon. He'd been of a mind to kill Fallon. But Fallon had fought him fair and had not taken advantage of him. Purley shuddered when he thought of what those red-hot rocks would have done to his face had Fallon let him fall into the pit at Beartrack.

But he had no qualms about killing Havenrite. And Libby deserved to see him die right in front of her eyes. In her own house. For Purley had seen Havenrite follow her up the trail. He knew what would happen the minute Libby spoke to Havenrite. Havenrite had a look in his eyes a man gets when a pretty woman leads the way.

It was very dark. Clouds whipped under the stars like a torn window shade.

At last he came to Libby's place. He dismounted a hundred yards from the house and carefully gauged the wind so he could approach from a direction where the horses would not catch his scent.

The window was bathed in lamplight. Two horses were in front, Libby's and Havenrite's. She hadn't even bothered to unsaddle, as she always did. Libby usually took care of her horses. Tonight she was in a hurry.

At the edge of the yard Purley removed his boots, and he went the rest of the way in his sock feet. For a moment he was afraid the horses had caught his scent. The big sorrel was tossing its head. Then it quieted. His hands were wet on the rifle.

He was against the house wall and he could hear a murmur of voices coming from inside. There was a metallic sound, a pot clanging on a stove lid.

"I don't need coffee with my whisky," Havenrite was saying in a pleased voice.

"I do." It was Libby.

"Come here. We're wasting time, Lib."

"I don't know whether I should have let you come here or not. After all—"

"I like you, Lib. I always have. You know that."

"Maybe I don't believe you."

"You shouldn't have busted up with me and took up with that thickheaded Purley."

"Jed was all right till he turned thief."

"And how about Kirk Fallon?"

Libby didn't say anything to that.

"I'm going to finish him, Lib. I'm breaking my men up into small bunches. I've given 'em orders. I don't want Fallon alive. I want him brought in—dead."

"I heard you," Libby said. "I was standing not ten feet

from you when you told them in front of the store."

Havenrite laughed. "I just wanted to make sure you heard."

"Coffee will be ready soon."

"Here, have a drink, Lib."

"No, you have one. I'll wait for the coffee." There was the sound of someone drinking from a bottle. Then Libby said, "I didn't like it much when I heard your version of why we quit going together."

Havenrite said, "A man's got to save his pride."

"At the expense of a woman's pride? You told it around that I quit you when you wanted to keep on like we were after you married Vanessa Berryman."

"You're not sore, Lib. You had a chance to think things over since we haven't been seeing each other. You've had Purley and Fallon and—"

"You make me sound like a prostitute."

"Hell, nothing like that."

"Tell me something, Rex."

"What?"

"I think you'd have hanged me that night."

"Not you, Lib. You got a lot of good years left in you. I want to be around to enjoy 'em." Havenrite sounded smug.

"There's no winning against you, Rex."

"You oughta know it by this time, Lib. Isn't that coffee done yet?"

"Looks like it." Libby's voice sounded strained all of a sudden, Purley noted, and he took a tighter grip on his rifle.

"Why did you care if Fallon showed up to collect from Berryman?" Libby was saying.

"I had things going right. I didn't want some stranger hanging around and messing things up. Say, why all this talk about Fallon and Berryman? The old man's dead, and Fallon—"

"Soon dead, is that it? Hold out your cup. Here's the coffee."

Havenrite's voice climbed in alarm: "Watch it!" A squall of pain burst from Havenrite's throat, and there was the sound of a kicked-back chair.

Then Libby was saying, "I'm going to do this country a favor. Before anybody else dies!"

"You haven't the guts to pull the trigger."

"No?"

There was the sound of bodies crashing together. A gunshot roared. The house window went dark.

Havenrite yelled, "Hank! Hank! See if there's anybody out there! I got this damn cat!"

"Not this cat you haven't got!" Libby cried.

Another gunshot and Havenrite yelled, "For God's sake, Lib!"

Purley had been starting for the front door when Havenrite yelled for Hank Ogden. Now he whirled as a sound off to the right caught his attention.

But he had no time to concentrate on this. The door was jerked open and Havenrite came plunging out through the front door. He crashed into Purley, who was just mounting the steps. The impact knocked Purley down. Hank Ogden was running up from the trees. The horses in front of the house were rearing, snorting.

A gun flamed from the door and Havenrite cried, "Hank, damn it! I dropped my gun!" Havenrite was scrambling around, trying to find the weapon he had lost in the collision with Purley.

Purley rose and leveled the rifle at Havenrite's head. But something streaked out from the darkness and he was aware of a terrible blow. The ground tilted up and struck him solidly in the face.

Unarmed, Havenrite sprinted for his horse and tore loose the reins as Libby, fortified behind the log house wall, began to fire a rifle. There were the sounds of two horses streaking away into the darkness.

"Jed, Jed!" Libby ran down the steps and put an arm under Purley's shoulder. He was too heavy, but at last he roused enough so he could help her get him into the house. He fell across the bed.

"I was going to kill him, Libby," he groaned. "In front of you. I wanted to get even."

"I might have known Rex wouldn't trust me," Libby said. She hadn't lighted the lamp. She had put on water to boil and was tearing up cloths for bandages. "He must have got word to Hank Ogden to follow him up here. Maybe he thought I was setting a trap."

"You did," Purley said weakly.

"Not a very good one. I spilled the coffee, but I was too close. He grabbed me."

"I guess Fallon means a lot to you, Libby. If you were going to kill a man over him—"

"Don't talk any more, Jed," Libby said, and probed the wound with her fingertips. She felt the hard outline of a bullet low on Purley's left side. "I'll heat a knife, Jed. I've got to get that bullet out. Can you stand it?"

"Yeah. Libby, I'm sorry for the things I said. And the way I acted. If I hadn't stole that money from Beartrack, would you have married me like you said?"

"Yes, Jed."

"Even if Fallon had come along anyhow?"

"Jed, when I'm married, I'm married all the way. Maybe most people wouldn't believe that about me."

"I sure mess things up," Jed groaned.

"No more than anybody else, Jed. The knife's hot. Grit your teeth."

"Will you kiss me first, Libby?"

"Sure."

"If I'd used my bone head we could have our two outfits together. We'd have a nice spread, Libby. And there's a future in the cow business."

"Tell me about it after I get this bullet out."

When this was done she was trembling and damp with perspiration. She went out into the yard and by lantern light hitched a team to her wagon. She somehow got Jed into the bed of the wagon.

Then she yelled into the darkness, "Beartrack, if you're out there, you'll have to kill a woman. Because I'm coming through!"

Only silence in the shadowed trees.

With a rifle on the seat she whipped up the team and drove recklessly down the grade in the direction of El Cobre and Doc Graham.

Chapter Nineteen

To KIRK FALLON his smartest move had been in shunting Vanessa Berryman aside. A man could not concentrate on a threatening danger if his thinking was clouded by an image; remembering how soft her lips had been, the way the sunlight struck her hair, the scent of lavender.

Kirk sipped from his glass of tequila. In his mind there was never any doubt of the outcome of his facing up to Havenrite—now that Vanessa was out of it. It was one of the qualities that had enabled him to survive the war and the violence in Mexico and the later turmoil of the cattle towns. A confidence in his ability, never allowing himself to think for an instant that he would not emerge the victor. He steadily drank tequila, but not too much, just enough to stave off exhaustion.

He had had little sleep and his body still had not fully recovered from the beating given him by the Beartrack men. And added to that was the punishment he had taken from Jed Purley's fists.

As he stood at the bar in the cantina and listened to the music and the sound of Spanish talk flow about him, he tried to dredge up a shred of grief from the shattered image of a man he had once admired—Sam Berryman.

Some things had been clarified when, in his last moments, Berryman related the story of a night of terror when he helplessly watched his older brother and the rest of the gold-seeking party being tortured to death by the Piutes. In the war he had seen men throw away their rifles in panic and run blindly to escape. But although he knew it happened, he could not understand it, even as he could not understand one partner deserting another in order to escape the possible return of marauding savages. Much as he might want to forgive Sam Berryman, he could not find it in his heart to do so.

Berryman had not been alone in his frantic efforts to made up for the fruitless years of war. There were thousands of men willing to bet on anything that would give them a stake in the ever growing frontier. Some were lucky; others looked their failure in the face and tried more direct methods with a mask and a gun.

And others, like Berryman, found whisky a ready companion when the trail became too rough. Looking back on it now, Kirk realized that in Mexico Berryman had known nothing of the business of raising horses. Kirk and Danny Dunster had carried him with their knowledge.

Here in El Cobre Valley, Sam Berryman had used his daughter's inheritance to buy a white elephant. Berryman had bought a beautiful stone house, and immaculate barns and corrals. And from the veranda he had an inspiring view of the mountains. But he had not bought himself a ranch.

And in order to save himself and his daughter, he had let Rex Havenrite do as he pleased.

The crowd in the Cantina de los Amigos thinned out. The dark-eyed Mexican girl who had smiled at him the night he made his escape here from the mob was behind the bar. Now and then she would give him a tentative smile, but he seemed intent on other matters. She would shrug and talk to the other customers.

Martínez, who owned the place, talked to Kirk, telling of the marvels of Chihuahua City, where he had been born. They spoke in Spanish, and Martínez, a great bear of a man with gray-black hair, would not let Kirk pay for the tequila. At last Martínez yawned and said he was going to catch some sleep. He told the girl, Carla, to keep the place open as long as Don Kirk Fallon cared to stay.

Finally he was the only customer. Carla set out a fresh glass and a shaker of salt for his tequila.

He kept staring at the street. The only lights across the plaza came from the lobby of the Lee House, and from Oberley's, on the opposite side of the street.

Then his ears caught the sound of a team at a hard run, and a wagon, coming along the main street from the direction of the Cobres. He went to the slatted swing doors and peered out. As the racing team and wagon passed the Lee House, he saw that the driver was a woman. Libby, he was sure of it.

Carrying his rifle, he turned to Carla. "If in fifteen minutes I am not back—"

"I will wait. It will be the wish of Martínez."

He hurried out, carrying his rifle. He saw the wagon skid around the corner a block north of the hotel.

He began to run, knowing that Libby's arrival in town at this time of night in a wagon meant that something had happened in the mountains.

As he rounded the corner he saw her pull up in front of Doc Graham's cottage, set back from the street. When she heard his running footsteps, she turned, bracing her feet, swinging up a rifle.

Then she recognized him. "It's Jed. He's been shot!" She told him what had happened at her place. "Kirk, when I came by Larnet's Store on my way down here, the pool had most of Havenrite's men disarmed."

"They weren't in that kind of mood when I last saw them."

"They waited until Havenrite had followed me up to my place, and then they got behind the Beartrack men and put rifles on them. They caught them by surprise. There are still about ten of the crew loose, but most of them are prisoners until this business is settled."

"So the pool showed some backbone," Kirk said, and saw that their loud talking had brought Doc Graham to the door with a lamp. He was a small man with mutton-chop whiskers. Kirk helped Jed Purley into the house. Purley seemed unable to speak, but he managed to give Kirk a tight smile.

While Doc Graham examined Purley, Kirk and Libby went outside.

"Rex gave the pool a great story about being neighborly," Libby said. "He blamed all the trouble on Sam Berryman."

"Berryman can't argue the point, that's for certain."

"Rex said that now that Berryman was dead, he'd leave the pool alone."

"And they believed him?"

"No. But they were so glad of a chance to ranch in peace for a spell, they didn't argue. It was Larnet who got them stirred up enough to tackle the Beartrack men. Not a shot was fired. Larnet said to tell you that you're not alone in this fight. He says for you to come up and they'll leave a few men to guard the Beartrack prisoners. The rest of them will join you and hunt down Havenrite. That Berryman shooting was plain murder. Rex can hang for it."

Kirk shook his head. "Havenrite will come here to town. I'll wait if it takes a week."

"Rex is in an ugly mood. He'll be twice as dangerous now."

"Who's with him?"

"Hank Ogden, but there are still some of the Beartrack crew that aren't accounted for."

Kirk said, "You better get a room at the hotel."

She shook her auburn head. "I'm staying here. In case Jed needs anything."

Kirk put a hand on her arm. "He's a good man."

"Yes, I suppose he is. I know he is." She turned for the house. "Don't try to do this alone. Go to Larnet's Store."

"I'll see."

"Promise me, Kirk."

Kirk shrugged and walked back toward the Cantina de los Amigos.

Rex Havenrite rode into El Cobre with Hank Ogden from the direction of Beartrack, keeping to side streets and alleys. Whenever he thought of Libby, he cursed. His right thigh pained. It was scalded where she had spilled the hot coffee on him. And he had lost his gun.

They slowed their horses as they passed the plaza. No one else was on the street. There was a lamp burning in the hotel lobby. Oberley's still showed a light. There were no horses at the rail.

Havenrite pulled up. "Give me your gun, Hank."

"But, Rex, I—"

"Give me your gun!"

"Why didn't you pick one up at Beartrack?"

"I had other things on my mind. Now hand it over, damn it!"

Reluctantly the black-bearded Ogden handed over his revolver butt first. Havenrite checked the loads and then hefted the gun a few times to get its balance.

"Go and see if Fallon's in the saloon."

Ogden rode up, stood in the stirrups to peer in the saloon window. He came back, shaking his head.

"Three of them fellas from the freight outfit playing poker. Nobody else."

Havenrite said, "Let's get a drink."

"You going to hunt for the girl?"

"Yeah," Havenrite grunted.

"Know where to find her?"

"I got an idea." Havenrite started his horse moving.

Ogden hung back. "You go ahead. I'm going over and see Carla."

"Someday you'll get your throat cut in them Mex joints. Don't stay all night. I might need you."

Ogden said nothing. This was not the time to argue with Rex. The less you said, the better. Rex had insisted they ride by Beartrack when they came down from the mountains. The Berryman girl wasn't there. Rex had searched the house, cussing out the servants, booting the men, threatening the women. But all they knew was that the girl had ridden out, weeping, after her father's body had been taken to town.

Ogden rode across the plaza and racked his horse in front of the Cantina de los Amigos. He looked through the slatted doors, and saw only Carla standing behind the bar, talking to a *vaquero.*

Ogden smoothed his beard, wished he'd had time for a trim and a haircut. His clothing was dusty and he felt like hell. Everything had gone wrong. Rex was a damn fool if he thought that pool bunch swallowed his story about Beartrack and them getting along. But he guessed Rex knew that himself. Rex was playing for time. By the time they'd got to Larnet's Store, Rex had cooled off. Berryman's getting shot had been something Rex hadn't counted on. Rex didn't figure to push things too hard right yet.

At Beartrack there had been only a few of the older hands, kept around for yard chores. They hadn't seen any of the rest of the crew. Ogden supposed they were off in the mountains hunting Kirk Fallon. If Fallon had any sense, he was probably right now heading for the Rim pass. When he thought of Fallon, he swore. Si Oldcamp had been his friend, and Fallon had killed him.

Ogden entered the cantina. Carla's eyes lighted up. She moved away from the *vaquero* she had been talking to, and came to Ogden. She set out a bottle and gave him both of her hands and smiled at him.

"You have not come here for so long," she said. "I think you do not like me."

"Sure I like you," Ogden said, and poured himself a drink. He felt naked without his gun. He had only the rifle in his saddle boot and a knife with a four-inch blade in a scabbard at his belt.

The *vaquero* finished his drink and went out, leaving Ogden alone with Carla at the bar.

Martínez stuck his gray-black head through a curtained doorway behind the bar and looked around his cantina. His eyes were heavy with sleep. He nodded to Ogden, then turned to Carla and spoke to her rapidly in Spanish.

Ogden's knowledge of the language was meager, but he had no trouble in catching the name of Kirk Fallon.

Carla said something more in Spanish and Martínez withdrew behind the curtained doorway. There was the sound of his weight settling on bedsprings.

Ogden looked at Carla, his eyes bright. "What about Fallon?"

Carla shrugged her bare shoulders. "He was here for hours," Carla said. "Drinking tequila. He and Martínez talked about Mexico. Martínez likes Fallon. He says there are few *yanquis* who talk the language like a Mexican." She flashed him a white smile. "We go now, eh?" She started to lead Ogden toward a stairway at the far end of the bar.

Ogden faced the street. "How long ago was he here?"

"Ten minutes, maybe. Why? He is not important. We are important, no?" She smiled with her white teeth and again tried to lead him toward the stairway.

Ogden went to the doors, peered through the slats, and stiffened when he saw a tall figure tramping across the plaza toward the cantina. It was Fallon, carrying a rifle.

Ogden stepped back, his mouth a hard line under the black beard. "Here he comes," he said tensely. "Get talking to him. Get close enough and get his gun. Understand? When you do, yell, and I'll come for him."

She looked at him in surprise. She shook her head. "No. You come here to see me, and that is right. But I do not mix in things that are not of my business."

Ogden swore and said, "Then get me a revolver. Martínez has likely got one."

But by this time the footsteps were louder outside, thumping now across the boardwalk. Ogden skirted the end of the bar and ducked down behind it out of sight.

Kirk Fallon entered, and instantly stiffened when he saw Carla's strained face. The girl stood with her back to the bar, her eyes wide.

Kirk came forward slowly until he stood in front of her, and a little to one side. "Who's back there?" he asked quietly, indicating the curtained doorway with a nod of his head. "Havenrite there?"

And at that moment Ogden came sailing over the bar, his boot heels striking Kirk in the chest. Kirk went down under the impact, rolled aside. Ogden flung himself forward. Lamplight caught the wicked gleam of a knife blade. Kirk ducked, and the blade, aimed at his throat, tore into the flesh of his right arm. He felt pain and blood and anger. As Ogden tumbled from the momentum of his lunge, Kirk scrambled to his feet. He reversed his rifle. As Ogden came up, Kirk smashed the man across the forehead with the rifle stock. Ogden dropped face down on the dirt floor and didn't move.

Carla stood woodenly, staring at Ogden. Martínez had been roused by the sound of the scuffle, and now he came into the front part of the cantina. He rubbed sleep from his eyes, then looked at Kirk's right shirt sleeve. It was blood-soaked.

"He cut you, the *cabrón,*" Martínez said.

Kirk said, "Have you got a bandage and a shirt I can borrow?"

"*Sí*, you wait." Martínez shouted at Carla to get water.

The girl hastened to obey. Some Mexicans living next door had heard the loud voices, and now they entered and stood around, talking among themselves and shaking their heads. Kirk had removed his shirt. The wound was not deep, he saw when the blood was washed off. He could use his arm. No tendons had been cut. But the arm was stiffening.

When the arm was bandaged and he had donned a blue wool shirt belonging to Martínez he took a long pull at a bottle of tequila. Ogden was beginning to stir. His forehead was swelling, turning purple.

Kirk reached down, jerked Ogden to his feet. The man sagged against the front of the bar, shaking his head. Then his eyes flickered open. They stayed open when he saw Kirk, and there was fear and a sullen defiance in them.

Kirk said, "Where's Havenrite?"

Ogden put a hand to the bruise on his forehead. "Ain't seen him."

"Libby Squires said you and Havenrite were together at her place."

"Rex went to Beartrack."

"Who came to town with you?"

"I come alone."

Kirk said, "How come you didn't try to shoot me in the back? Why a knife."

"Because I wanted to cut you up. You killed Si. He was my best friend."

Kirk let his eyes rove over the stocky, black-bearded man. He saw the empty holster. "Lose your gun?"

"Yeah, and the hell with you, Fallon."

Kirk looked at Martínez and said in Spainsh. "Can you lock him up?"

"*Sí*, in the storeroom," Martínez answered, and led the way through the curtained doorway. In the alley behind the cantina there was a door. Martínez unlocked it. There was a room there, where he kept supplies. Ogden was shoved inside. The door was locked.

"You be careful," the Mexican said. "That arm is not good. You cannot draw the pistol."

Kirk was looking across a weed-grown lot, bathed in moonlight. He could see the two-story white house where he had left Vanessa.

He turned to Martínez. "I'll be all right. Just keep Ogden here."

Chapter Twenty

KIRK SKIRTED the cantina and kept to back alleys until he came to Oberley's. The town was quiet, sleeping. Not even a dog barked at the moon, which had come out from behind a cloudbank. In the distance the jagged teeth of the Cobres bit into the purple sky. Stars were very bright. A drunk lurched along the boardwalk, weaving, singing under his breath.

Kirk turned to the right and moved soundlessly up on the veranda of the saloon. A glance through the front window showed Oberley, standing rigid behind the bar, his long face bloodless. He was alone.

Kirk stepped in, put his back to the wall. The swing doors squeaked on their unoiled hinges, and then were still.

Oberley just looked at him.

Kirk said, "Havenrite been here?"

The saloonman nodded. He seemed too frightened to speak. Perspiration showed through his thinning hair and along the part.

Kirk glanced around the room. Cards littered one of the tables. There was a cigar smoking at an edge of the table where someone had gone off and left it.

"Where'd everybody go?"

"Havenrite told 'em to clear out. They did. Only three fellas from the Acme freight outfit. They didn't want to tangle with Rex."

Kirk felt a nerve twitch at a corner of his mouth. "You better tell me, Oberley. Where's Havenrite?"

"He— I think he went to the hotel."

Kirk saw the strain on the man's face, the trembling lips, the shine of perspiration. Kirk suddenly ducked so that he was covered by the bar, and skirted one end. He got behind Oberley. There was a small room behind the bar Kirk, gun in his left hand, peered around a corner of the door-frame. The room was empty.

Kirk came to stand beside Oberley. The back of the man's shirt was damp with perspiration. Kirk's heart was pounding. The drunk he had seen on the street came floundering through the swing doors, and lurched up to the bar.

"Gimme a drink, Oberley."

Oberley found his voice. "You've had enough, Jim. Go home and sleep."

Jim was already asleep, his short body bowed forward, head on the bar lip. He was snoring. In a minute he would fall down and maybe hit his head on the brass rail. Kirk steered him to the door. The man weaved off down the street into the darkness.

Kirk turned. "Havenrite's put the fear in you. But he's through in this country and I think he knows it. Tell me where he is."

Oberley closed his eyes and stared down at his fingers, locked at the edge of the bar. "I—I—" He couldn't get it out.

Then Kirk felt an unreasoning rage. "You told him, didn't you? You told him where Vanessa is."

Oberley's tongue shot out, moistening his lower lip. "I had to, Fallon."

"Damn you, Oberley!"

Kirk, carrying his rifle, started for the door, but Oberley ran and caught him by an arm. "Don't go to my house. For God's sake, don't go there!"

"If Havenrite gets his hands on that girl—"

Oberley sprang in front of him and barred the doors by flinging wide his arms. His eyes were frantic. "Havenrite said if I told anybody where he'd gone, my wife—well, she might get hurt."

Kirk pushed him aside. "How'd he figure you'd know where the girl was staying?"

"Rex knew my wife and Vanessa were friendly. About the only woman friend the girl has in town."

Kirk felt a rising impatience. "Your wife isn't going to get hurt," he said.

"Your arm, Fallon. What's happened to your arm?"

Kirk looked. The knife cut had bled through the shirt sleeve.

Perhaps in the dark Havenrite wouldn't notice.

Kirk lifted the revolver from its holster and felt a stab of pain in his arm. He replaced it. He was sweating.

There were sudden footsteps outside, a man's and a woman's. Kirk stepped back, put his rifle against the wall, and waited. The swing doors opened and Vanessa Berryman came in, laughing. Havenrite was looking down at her and smiling.

Havenrite nodded to Kirk and said, "Vanessa, you go sit at a table. It isn't ladylike for you to be at the bar. Oberley, I want you to make us up some meat sandwiches. And we'll take a few bottles of beer with us. And yeah, a bottle of whisky for me."

Oberley stood as if frozen to the floor.

Outside in the darkness somewhere the drunk began to sing. A window banged up in the hotel across the street and somebody yelled, "Kee-ryst sake! Shut up!" The window shut with a clatter.

Havenrite looked at Oberley. "Get a move on, man." He went over and held a chair for Vanessa. She sat down. Her lips were bloodless but wore a fixed smile, as if Havenrite had said something funny outside.

Kirk said, "This man kills your father and you laugh at his jokes." He moved his rifle nearer the door.

She did not look at him, and for a moment made no reply. Then, her voice under control, she said, "The shooting of my father was an accident."

"Vanessa and I are going over to the county seat and get married," Havenrite said. "That right?" He looked at the girl. He was big and tough-looking. He needed a shave.

Vanessa said, "That's right."

Kirk shook his head. "This makes no sense. He's holding something over your head."

"I'm going of my own free will," she said, but this time Kirk detected a faltering in her voice.

Havenrite pushed Oberley around the end of the bar. "Your wife is safe enough—for now. But I saw our friend Fallon here lock Hank Ogden up. And I made Martínez let him out. Ogden's over at your house. Oberley, watching your wife. If there's any trouble here—" Havenrite spread his hands. "Hank's in a sour mood and he's likely to do anything. He's got a swollen head."

Oberley's reserve broke. "Goddamn you, Rex. I won't take this!"

Havenrite turned and said, "You'll take it. And so will everybody else around here. Vanessa and I are going to run Beartrack the way we want it run. Not the way her father wanted to run it."

Oberley, his hands trembling, set out some bottles of cool beer and a bottle of whisky. "I got no meat for sandwiches."

Havenrite shrugged. "No matter. Put the bottles in a sack. We got to be moving. Got to hire a buggy."

Oberley got a gunny sack and put the bottles of beer and the whisky into it. Then he put the bag on the bar. Havenrite did not immediately pick it up.

Kirk stood with his back against the wall. His shoulders ached, so great was the tension in him. The drunk outside had stopped singing. It was so quiet that his ears hurt.

"Vanessa," he said, his voice calm enough, "step outside. Havenrite and I have something to finish. Just the two of us." Kirk's mouth twisted. "Unless, of course, he thinks he can outshoot me."

A bug thumped against one of the overhead reflectors. The girl sat stiffly in the chair, and Havenrite said, "I'm willing to give you this chance to ride out of El Cobre, Fallon—alive. For her sake. Don't press your luck."

"Go outside, Vanessa," Kirk repeated, and stood a little away from the wall now, his long legs loose, right hand poised above his gun. He looked at his rifle, leaning against the wall, wanting to place it in case it should be needed.

Tension mounted. Havenrite was studying him out of his amber eyes. He had to bluff Havenrite until the girl got to a place of safety. For he could hear someone creeping along the alley beside the saloon, and a named flashed across his mind—Hank Ogden.

Havenrite moved his lips, pressing them together, putting lines of pressure at the corners of his mouth. His head was cocked as if he too heard the sound. "I can handle you, Fallon," he said, and his gaze flicked in the direction of the sound in the alley, then back to Kirk.

Vanessa stood up and looked across the room at Kirk, who stood rigid near the door. "You've got to understand that I'm going to marry Rex. I don't love him now, but maybe I will in time." She took a step toward Kirk. "Maybe I don't like the way things have turned out. But I've had money all my life. I couldn't be a pauper, Kirk." Her eyes seemed very dark in her pale face.

"Rex says he can save Beartrack," she went on, moving another step toward him, "and I believe him." There was a faint beading of perspiration on her bruised upper lip. The perspiration must have stung the cut, for she lifted a hand to her mouth. "Rex and I are rough on each other," she said. "He hit me, but look what I did to his face."

She looked across the room at Havenrite, at the marks on his face left by her nails. He wasn't looking at her. He was poised on the balls of his feet, staring at the fingers of Kirk's right hand.

There were drops of blood rolling down the length of the fingers, dripping from the nails to form bright spots on the dirt floor.

Havenrite lifted his eyes to Kirk's face, and smiled. "Hurry up, Vanessa. I can't wait to settle with this gunfighting man!"

And Vanessa saw the blood at that moment. And so did Oberley, standing behind his bar. The saloonman seemed to die a little.

Vanessa said, "Good luck, Rex," and started through the door, but at that moment she whirled and snatched up Kirk's rifle from where it was leaning against the well. "Ogden's outside!" she cried, and worked the lever of the rifle to send a bullet into the chamber.

Kirk had felt the blood on his fingertips, but had not dared to take his eyes from Havenrite and glance down.

Oberley yelled, "Look out, Fallon!"

Kirk had tried to throw himself against Vanessa, to knock her to the floor and away from danger. But she was too swift, and she was out the door. He could hear her high-heeled boots clattering across the veranda.

Havenrite drew and fired, and a great gout of hard-packed earth was ripped from the floor and flung into Kirk's face. Despite the pain of his bad arm, Kirk got his gun free. He went to his knees, rolled as Havenrite fired again. Kirk felt a numbing shock in his left foot.

Outside there was the crash of a rifle and a man's hoarse scream. Havenrite looked toward the door, surprised.

Transferring the gun to his left hand, Kirk got off a shot that staggered Havenrite.

The crash of weapons in the thick-walled room was deafening. Gun smoke swirled in thick black clouds. Havenrite was crouched in front of the bar, bringing the palm of his left hand in a downstroke across the hammer of his gun. Kirk rolled, came to his knees, felt the breath of the bullet past his face. He steadied his nerves and fired his revolver, and fired it again.

Kirk saw Havenrite lurch toward him, the gun sagging. "Damn you, Fallon, damn you!" And he pitched forward, bleeding at the mouth.

Kirk got to his feet and nearly lost his balance. He found that Havenrite had shot off the heel of his left foot.

Kirk limped to Havenrite, got the man's gun, and put it on the bar. "Keep an eye on him, Oberley," he warned, and limped outside.

He found Vanessa on the veranda steps, weeping. The rifle was at her side. In the street a black-bearded man lay face down. Lights were springing up in windows. Windows in the hotel were opening. People were looking out. The clerk came to the lobby door, turned, and shouted to somebody inside. The hostler came running down from the Atlas Stable. Mexicans were streaming across the plaza in various stages of undress.

Kirk went down into the street and turned Hank Ogden over on his back. There was a hole in the center of the swelling on his forehead. A crowd gathered around the dead man in the street, and others were pushing into the saloon.

Oberley came to the veranda, his face white. "Havenrite's dead." He looked back over his shoulder. "Somebody look after the place. I'm going down to see if my wife's all right."

"You don't have to worry about her," Vanessa said, wiping tears on the back of her hand. She put her head on Kirk's chest. "Rex was on the porch of the Oberley house when he saw you lock Ogden up. He had a gun out and said he would shoot you in the back if I didn't agree to what he said. So I did. But there's no dishonor in not keeping your word to a man like Rex."

Kirk said, "You should go to Santa Fe, and when you come back—"

"Kirk, Beartrack's gone. I know that. But can't we start —together?"

"I've got a ranch in the mountains. It's not much now, but someday it will be. I think Bert Wingate will see that you get something out of Beartrack, and—"

"Take me home, Kirk."

"There's no house there. Only a burned cabin."

"Then we'll live in a tent until we can build one."

"I should marry you first."

"Then why don't you?"

Oberley handed Kirk the sack he had made up for Havenrite. "Go hire a buggy. You ought to be at the county seat before the beer gets too warm."

THE END

of a novel by

Dudley Dean